Eric's Choice

'Violet? Are you there, Violet?'

No reply. He went into the kitchen. As he'd expected, used dishes everywhere. The sink was full of pans. In Spain they had eaten *cordon bleu* food. Once home she bought ready-cooked meals.

'Violet? I'm back.'

Her purse was on the dresser, typical of her carelessness. He counted thirty pounds. He'd given her eighty this morning. How long would her spending go on? Was she in the downstairs cloakroom? Be there, Violet, be there.

'Violet? I'm back again. I'm afraid I may have upset you. I want to apologize.'

He'd go down on his knees, eat dirt, anything, if she would just be there.

Eric's Choice

Ursula Holden

METHUEN

A Methuen Paperback

ERIC'S CHOICE

British Library Cataloguing in Publication Data

Holden, Ursula
  Eric's choice.
  I. Title
  823'.914[F]   PR6058.O434

  ISBN 0-413-55650-6

First published in Great Britain 1984
by Methuen London Ltd
Copyright © 1984 by Ursula Holden
This edition published 1986
by Methuen London Ltd
11 New Fetter Lane, London EC4P 4EE

Printed and bound in Great Britain by
Richard Clay (The Chaucer Press) Ltd,
Bungay, Suffolk

And did the Countenance Divine
Shine forth upon our clouded hills?
And was Jerusalem builded here . . .

William Blake

CHAPTER ONE

Eric

Now that he was alone he admitted that he'd lost his temper. Violet's childish and disgusting behaviour had driven him to violence. He shuddered when he remembered. The cold weather and his own self-disgust made him feel debilitated. She wouldn't walk out and leave him, she wouldn't dare, she needed him too much. Besides, she felt the cold. One of the things he used to love about her was the coldness of her nose, he used to love kissing it; her nose was as cold as a cat's. He'd not kissed any of her for months.

But he refused to feel any remorse. They had shouted at each other before, doubtless they would again. Tonight had been different, tonight he had lost control and nothing excused violence, whatever the provocation. Had she wanted it? She had mocked him with her eyes as well as with words. 'You animal. You ought to be on four legs.'

She was so beautiful, as beautiful now as she'd been a year ago when he'd first seen her singing in the school choir. Those pure eyes, as guileless as if they'd been rinsed, had looked up at him and he'd been lost. But her eyes lied, she was a living lie. He soon found that out, after his ring was on her hand. If only he'd left her where she was, living in pig ignorance. She didn't fit into his life, or the house on the green, she couldn't and wouldn't change. He should have known, with that barnyard background of hers, but he'd seen her singing 'Jerusalem' and become helpless.

She'd had a reputation for idleness, he'd learned that from the members of staff who had taught her. Violet Stubbs was all show, no substance, further school education would be wasted on her. She had told him quite openly that work didn't appeal to her and his offer of marriage did. She fancied being kept. Her mother had been even more eager: she had brought Violet up strictly, no living together, no pre-marital sex, she had kept her Violet pure for marriage. As far as he was concerned he wanted her on any terms. And so beautiful Violet became his and demonstrated to him what true idleness was. She was spendthrift too, her rinsed blue eyes had only to light on something costly, ugly and tasteless and she must have it. His house was quite crammed with her ugly objects, her ugly sounds, ugly evidence of her existence. She still remained beautiful, though, whatever she wore.

At first, bemused with love, he had smiled at whatever she did; her extraordinary tastes and her extravagances were touching, she actually seemed to prefer what was debased and third rate. His house had become a travesty of its former self. Her music, her perfume, even her voice that had once charmed him jarred now. She left the g's from word endings, she rarely pronounced an h. And her vowel sounds!

Tonight she had actually said she was leaving. She must not do that, he'd put a stop to it. He had left the house first, before she did. He willed her to stay in the house until he got back. He'd soon talk her round. He would apologize, he would placate her. As he had left she shouted out that he needn't think she would stay because he was getting out first. She hated this sodding house, he was welcome to it. He had heard her through the double glazing as he'd hurried down the path. She was the animal, not him. No wonder they had no friends. How could he take a wife like that to the school functions? As the English literature master he had a reputation to maintain. The one time he had taken her to a sixth form play she had yawned all evening, had filed her nails and scratched herself. Every time she opened her mouth she mutilated what he most admired, his own language beautifully expressed.

Tonight he had walked out of the house, out of range of sneers and jibes. He hated to think of those eyes. He'd been walking for hours round the green. The night was sharp with frost. Well, he refused to feel depressed or resentful. Anyone would think him a criminal, sneaking into the night. He was normal, any man would have done as he had. He must stay unemotional.

The green looked blacker at night, as if the blackness of his mood had spread. The tree branches were huge, black shapes over the grass. There were no couples tonight, the lovers were all inside. Lovers? He and Violet had loved once, deeply, meaningfully. 'My wife and my love,' he used to say.

He dared not go back. He was afraid. What would he find? Under different circumstances he would have liked solitude: he didn't want to live alone. He was used to her, had done everything he could to provide for her. What had she done for him? He was worn out emotionally as well as physically. He wanted another bath. He'd been walking for over two hours, the frost had crept through his shoe soles, he'd forgotten his scarf. He looked up. A beautiful night, starry, without a wind. There was the milky way, a pale splash to his right. How reassuring the heavens were, the firmament didn't change. When life was bitter you only had to look up at the constellations.

The trouble with Violet was her total lack of any kind of sensitivity, and her uninterest in the things he cared about. She didn't understand exclusivity. She didn't understand his nature. He might appear confident on the outside, as a teacher it was necessary, he had to be. Inside he was quite shy. The right sort of wife would appreciate this. She was so brash, in spite of her innocent eyes. She was coarse-mouthed, filthy-minded, obtuse; why then did he need her?

His right hand ached, he couldn't feel his feet now. He

9

would walk once more round the green, hurrying where the trees were thick. As he walked up the garden path he strained to hear sounds of her, loud pop music usually. All the lights were burning. He put his key in the outer door. The lock grated. The inner door was locked too. Quiet inside, no radio or taped muzak. Sometimes she played both at once. He felt for his smaller key. Silence. He had complained so often about her cacophony, he would be glad of it now. The hall smelled as it always did, that smell that he once had loved.

After eleven months of breathing the smell of violets it had lost all its allure. Sometimes it made him choke. In Spain he had bought her colognes, fresh tangy scents which she had sniffed without interest before rubbing on more violet stuff. It had to be violets to match her name, a name that he'd like her to change. What about Viola, from the Latin, favoured by Shakespeare, less commonplace than Violet? She had answered this suggestion with her usual bluntness. She'd been christened Violet and Violet she would stay, okay? She didn't fancy a change, not for him or anyone. Her name was a misnomer, she was violent, brassy, rude, and her clothes matched her. Her mother, or Ivy as she preferred to be called, had always spoiled her. When he first met Violet she hadn't owned a passable garment and now, almost a year later, her clothes were even worse. Only now they were extravagantly priced. The house stank of her. Everything was coloured purple. What an extremist she was!

He tried to understand her, to suffer her vagaries until she became adjusted to her new position. He had even encouraged her to make changes, to buy what she liked for the house which was hers now as well as his. As mistress of the corner house on the green, he wanted her to have a say. His wife and his love, he wanted her happiness most. He hadn't expected to be taken so literally, hadn't realized her tastes were so outrageous. Yet he still wanted her. If only he didn't he wouldn't be so upset now. She was like a sickness that didn't improve.

10

He had started out with admirable intentions, he hoped to mould her to his ways, change her. She'd changed all right, she became more shocking, more tawdry by the week. Her nightdresses were little more than scraps of swansdown and sequins, she rarely wore knickers at all. Recently she had been dyeing her hair purple and combing it into spikes. She chewed gum, metal baubles hung from her ears, she wore razor blades round her neck. Once she had changed the house, she lost interest in everything but her appearance. She had become lazy, had taken to insulting him, with a nasty gleam in her eyes. At seventeen she still thought like a child.

She'd been fifteen when he'd first seen her singing in assembly. 'Till we have built Jerusalem, in England's green and pleasant land.' Hers had been the shortest skirt, the lowest neckline, hers the spikiest heels. Her left eye tooth protruded from her row of white teeth, her eyes were remarkably blue. He'd taken one look and wanted her. 'William Blake would have been charmed by your rendition,' he had said.

She had given him her rinsed blue stare. 'Eh? Talk English can't you?'

After making enquiries about her in the staffroom, learned what his colleagues thought about her, he saw himself as her saviour. It was ordained from above. He would marry her if that was the only way to get her.

Her mother, Ivy, had presented no obstacles, quite the reverse. Violet herself hadn't been clamorous. 'Eh? You want me that much? Okay.' She had told him she'd like a posh house to do as she liked in. She was sick of home. It was cold. At that time he'd have promised her the galaxy. He'd found his house on the green without difficulty, a perfect setting for his perfect girl.

His own mother, Charmian, had reservations from the start but she hadn't stood in his way. Dear Charmian, she'd even helped him, donating furniture from their old home. Thanks to Charmian the house on the green was fully furnished before he and Violet moved in. Charmian had perfect taste. His sense of elegance had been learned from her. He and Violet had returned from their Spanish honeymoon to a perfectly appointed house. Antique furniture, a few Persian rugs, good lighting, some Victorian water-colours on the washed pastel walls. But Violet had other ideas it soon transpired, and the changes began. He'd promised her a free rein; he couldn't go back on his word.

First she changed the house name. What had previously been a number depicted in roman numerals became 'Purple Rest'. The white paintwork turned purple, she stuck purple plastic hydrangea into the flowerbeds in front. The day came when he got back from school to find most of the furniture gone. The objects she had bought in replacement were so ugly that he'd winced. He'd tried to remonstrate. He had meant that she should stick to the existing style and period; Charmian had gone to such pains. It had been a mistake to mention Charmian. Violet had been most rude. He wanted her to be happy, didn't he? Well then, she'd buy what she sodding liked. He'd given way to her. That mouth, those rinsed blue eyes, that smile with the jutting eye tooth were his, that's all that mattered. His mistress, his wife, his love.

That first time he'd taken her out he'd looked down the neck of her blouse while she told about the strictness at home. Her Dad and Ivy were tartars, home was cold, she loathed school. She wanted to get away from both places. Her curved fingers had touched his wrist, had moved downwards to his hand. She scrutinized his hand, then she questioned. How had he hurt it? The girls in her class wondered about it. Had he been born like that? Was he embarrassed? She had shown no reticence, didn't know the meaning of tact, she was insistent, tipping her face up to his. He mustn't be shy about it. Tell her. His right hand was just like a pen. Did it feel rotten only having six fingers all told? Still, his thumbs were okay, that was something.

He had pulled back from her, hot, uneasy. The last thing he

wished to discuss was his hand but he wanted her to touch him, her touching was thrilling. He tried to turn the subject towards books. She'd interrupted, she had no time for books; his hand, though, talk about that. How long had it been that queer shape? Did it hurt? Okay then, she got the message, he was shy. Talk about his Mum, how did he feel about her? She had known from the start how to disturb him, how to probe into delicate areas. He had counter-questioned. She must tell him about her family first.

She had lived in Shadwell all of her life, in the Peabody flat where her grandparents had lived. Her father ran a gift stall and travelled round the markets, London outskirts mostly. Souvenirs and knick-knacks were his speciality, a nice little moveable shop. Summer and early spring were his best times, when the Americans came. Most tourists loved the queen. He did a nice line in Buckingham Palace models, small statues of the royals. He had a van, his was a one-man-show. She used to help him as a little kid. He wanted her to get trained for something, there wasn't any work that she fancied, though. She used to like playing shops. She loved her Dad and she loved Ivy, only they were both too strict. School was dead boring, surely he agreed? 'Course he only taught sixth form girls, the toffee noses, the ones with all the brain. What was his own Dad doing? Oh? Pity. She had guessed that he might be dead. So he lived alone with his Mum? Shame really, not having a Dad. All the girls in her class talked about him. She couldn't wait to leave school.

Three months later she was sixteen and she was his wife. Up to the last Ivy had enforced the curfew. He hadn't seen Violet naked, hadn't put his hand inside her clothes, nor even his tongue in her mouth. He'd not objected. A wife like Violet was worth waiting for. His beautiful wife, his love.

Though Charmian had taught him so much she rarely gave advice. 'Use your own judgement,' she always said. She had said what she thought about Violet. 'If you marry that girl you will rue it. You'll be alone, you'll be lonely.' Blinded with love he'd been convinced that all he needed was Violet. His father-in-law, Chester, a dry man with a leathery face, hadn't approved either. Ivy wanted the marriage; she usually got her way.

Violet couldn't help her background. He had been to Shadwell, seen the flat, refusing to feel daunted. Those people were the salt of the earth. Charmian refused to meet them but with her usual generosity she had made the house ready for when they returned from Spain. 'Furnished down to a teaspoon, my sweet, don't say I haven't tried.' She kept away. She never uttered Violet's name. She referred to her as 'the waif'. She'd made her point, they didn't mix, it was best to stay apart. The only time she had come to the house was a time better forgotten.

Violet wasted no time, she started to turn the house into a kind of palace of fun. Each day after school he was afraid of what he might find. Wallpaper patterned with violets the size of rabbits appeared on the pastel walls. Overstuffed chairs, virulent nylon carpets instead of parquet and Persian rugs. His Meissen, his Sitzendorf figurines by seaside souvenirs. There was an effigy of the royal wedding couple made of sponge. There was Big Ben made of pipe cleaners. Instead of his beautiful Victorian water-colours were tea towels depicting animals with grinning faces. He avoided the dining-room now; it had been his favourite room. He tried to be lenient, she knew no better, she was her parents' child. But surely Ivy didn't leave lights on, or taps running, or allow food to go bad?

He put his keys in his pocket, breathing anxiously. He hung his coat up. The heat in the hall was intense. Violet scent choked him again. Never mind, he wanted her, he would stay loyal whatever the cost. She was probably asleep, in one of those preposterous nightgowns. She had an off-beat charm, she was unusual. He longed for a sight of that face.

'Violet? Are you there, Violet?'

No reply. He went into the kitchen. As he'd expected, used dishes everywhere. The sink was full of pans. In Spain they had eaten *cordon bleu* food. Once home she bought ready-cooked meals.

'Violet? I'm back.'

Her purse was on the dresser, typical of her carelessness. He counted thirty pounds. He'd given her eighty this morning. How long would her spending go on? Was she in the downstairs cloakroom? Be there, Violet, be there.

'Violet? I'm back again. I'm afraid I may have upset you. I want to apologize.'

He'd go down on his knees, eat dirt, anything, if she would just be there.

The shower curtains were pulled back, the mauve lavatory was bare. Under the toilet roll was a tampon box. He used to know her menstrual cycle, he used to remember her dates. Had . . . what he'd done . . . had he hurt her? It wasn't entirely his fault. She was so icy, she'd become so remote, not letting him touch her now, not touching him.

He went to the back door. Locked and bolted. He looked out into the yard. There were his socks on the washing line, stiff-frosted in the dark. Her plastic bird bath had ice on it, where no birds ever came. Gnomes and Disney creatures stared with mocking eyes and grins. No, Violet and he didn't have any friends, Charmian had been right. He didn't have even Violet now. She lacked taste, she was rude, she was ignorant, she threw away valuable things. She didn't cook for him, she was idle, she dressed in a trollopy way. She was . . . what was she? Magic. His beautiful wife, his love.

A cat howled in the distance, the other side of the wall.

'Puss? Here puss. Is that you, Dick?'

It wasn't Dick's miaow. He called again. Then he shut the door, bolting it. He'd forgotten all about Dick. Dick had started the trouble tonight. If Dick was in the house now it meant Violet would come back. She wouldn't abandon it, she was too fond of Dick. He put his hand under the sofa and chairs, he groped. No cat, but another purse of purple embroidered silk. He'd bought it in Spain for her, a symbol, a token of their love. 'I know it's sentimental, Violet, but we'll keep kisses in it. We'll always keep it filled.' She had enchanted him, she was a witch, she taught him, he taught her. Love was instinctive, the kissing, the being kissed. Love was insatiable, exploring each crease and cranny, kissing, feeling, licking. They had drunk champagne, exchanging it mouth to mouth, blending together, sucking. How he longed for the taste of her at this moment, her saliva, the feel of her teeth. They had fought over the kissing purse, now it lay forgotten, pushed under a chair, dust in its mauve stitching. Spain had been an idyll. They had learned about love together. Life went sour as soon as they got back. Was it something to do with this house?

He threw the purse down. The drawing-room felt dead. If she'd return he would never complain or criticize again. He forced himself to look in the dining-room where her ruinous touch was worst. It was a bar now, with more tea towels, more purple plastic flowers. Her pride was her plastic piano. It played 'God Save the Queen' when you pressed a switch. There was a spittoon that squirted water and a brass cannon that shot flames. He groaned and shut the door. He called up the stairs.

'Violet? Dick? Are you there?'

He went up. The smell of violets in their bedroom was even thicker. The puce-toned sheets were strewn sideways, her nightdress was under the bed. He touched the swansdown and sequins, the lace felt slightly warm. A tuft of fur clung to a sequin, the material looked clawed. There was a patch of damp. He sniffed. Ugh.

He'd never wanted a cat, her idea, the filthy dribble-mouthed thing. Though he had secretly hoped that something alive might make her more affectionate towards him, more like she'd been in Spain. She barely spoke except to ask for more cash. Neither of them cared about children. He'd asked her again recently. 'Another Mummy's boy like you? No thanks, I'd sooner look after Dick,' had been her reply.

The cat had started things off tonight. Any man would object to a cat in his bed, night after night, salivating over the pillow. It snuggled into Violet like a human, pushing him into the cold. Animals should stay on the floor or outside. Cats had fleas in their fur, they got worms, they were intimate with their tongues. They sniffed things. He had tried to put up with it for her sake; the cat pleased her, he'd been patient. That night, starved of physical and mental intimacy, he had reached for her in despair, wanting her kisses, wanting the feel of her face. He'd encountered a wet whiskered mask, he'd felt the bite of teeth. He'd shouted and switched on the lamp. Not his wife's dear blue eyes but two yellow ones. Dick had opened his mouth and hissed. The devil. He could catch tetanus or rabies. He had hit out and missed the cat, he hadn't meant to hit her. Violet screamed, leave her alone. Get out. Sleep somewhere else. He'd lost control completely. Her lazy ways, her extravagance, her unspeakable commonness made her unfit to live. Bitch. Trollop. Cur. She had opened her mouth wide, her sharp teeth and pointed tongue grinned. Go on. Hit her again, that's all he was fit for. Wife beater. He had seized her purple hair and pulled it, had hit her again and again. He had pulled up her nightdress, flung her out of the bed. On the floor he had tried to straddle her, he'd fought to unlock her legs. She had thrashed, scratched, shrieked. He had got her throat with his left hand, with his right he had prodded and jabbed.

She got away, she was leaving him, she'd had all she would take. He had rushed after. She must not leave the house. He'd go, she must stay, she mustn't go out in the cold. 'Go if you want. But I ain't staying. You animal. You ought to be on four legs.' The look in her eyes alarmed him, her jutting eye tooth looked fierce.

He dropped the torn nightdress on the bed again. He wanted

his wife and his love.

Downstairs in the kitchen the mauve feeding dish and drinking bowl were licked clean. He unbolted the back door again, looking out at the frosted socks.

'Dick? Are you there, Dick? I'm back.'

CHAPTER TWO

Violet

She leaned forward, holding Dick tightly. The taxi smelled of soot. She whispered into the whiskers, sharp against her mouth and cheeks. Dick was a real true friend. Real friends didn't want you to change, they took you as you were. She wanted Shadwell and the buildings again where she'd been born and raised. She'd left because it was old fashioned and Ivy was too strict. She couldn't wait to get back.

All this would end up in court very likely and serve Eric right if it did. Thug. Creep. Animal. Just wait until Ivy heard. Ivy was old fashioned about marriage, said it was for life. You made a promise, you stuck to it. 'Course she was a Catholic too – at least she was when it suited her, when it came to sex, babies or divorce. Ivy had said grab Eric, him being a teacher, posh spoken, with class. To Ivy he'd been a fine gentleman with a lovely house on the green. Ivy knew nothing about the rows though.

Spain had been nice, so lovely. She'd thought living in the house would be too. Eric had changed. When they got back he stopped fussing her up, stopped admiring her and started picking holes. Early marriage was fine for the likes of her parents. Dad didn't nag at Ivy or try to change her; Ivy did nothing wrong.

She'd rung home after Eric banged out of the house. 'I'm coming over now.' They'd be wondering, they'd be excited, she was always welcome at home whatever the time, day or night. She'd just grabbed Dick and left the house, been lucky a taxi came. She'd a fiver in her pocket to pay. Must be the coldest night of the year. She liked the hot pipes and comfort at 'Purple Rest'. With Ivy and Dad there was another kind of warmth. They loved you, that's what it was.

'Purple Rest' had been exciting at first, she liked making changes, making it all look nice. She got bored with it after that, and Eric hated it. But she couldn't live there as it was, with that old stuff, old rugs, everything ever so plain. He'd said to buy what she liked and she had. Then he'd criticized. He'd given her the world in Spain, no favour was too much. Now he just sneered at her. She'd sooner be on her own. Living with him was as good as being alone. He barely spoke, he made her feel stupid and cheap. She wished he'd go away, him and his papers and books. The girls in 'C' stream used to laugh at him. So glum, and that hand like a pen. Shy too. 'Course she blamed Charmian for a lot of it, she had brought him up all wrong. Being shy didn't mean you had a kind nature and Charmian wasn't kind either. She smiled a lot, but not inside, she never smiled with her eyes. She blamed Charmian for Eric's hand, taking pills before he was born. Sleeping pills most probably, or perhaps she'd got depressed. Eric wouldn't have a word said against Charmian, thought the sun shone from her bum. She had thought his hand was quite sweet first, with one finger and the thumb on his wrist. It sickened her now, especially after tonight. If only he'd understand her. Why did he want her to change? They'd been happy in Spain, Spain was beautiful. The only time he looked at her now was to complain. She'd done her hair purple to make him notice her, spent hours on it, with soap, dye, gum. Most probably Dad wouldn't like it either, but Ivy would only laugh. Ivy was strict but she did laugh and she liked the telly, liked musicals and singing old songs. The whole thing was a cock-up really, her marriage to Eric. Yes, she blamed Charmian for a lot. Charmian had tried to spoil their wedding too, peering about, then going away. She was stuck up and boring and looked it. A proper toe-rag she'd picked for a mother-in-law.

That time in Spain, so lovely, flying off through the sky, the kissing, drinking wine, and bed. He'd wanted to please her, worried about her, wanted to know what she liked. She was his joy, his delight, his wonder, now she was a trollop or a cur. That first time with him had been like flying, she'd lost control of her hands. She'd cried out, called his name, moaned. She'd never done it before. She'd asked afterwards why her legs were wet and pools of it in the bed. He'd been proud of himself: she had culminated, rather unusual, first time. 'Culminated? Talk English, can't you?' she'd answered, and wanted to try it again. They'd drunk a lot of wine there, and spent time round the gift shops. He'd bought her things in fancy arcades. What happened to that kissing purse? Not that she cared now. Mad sod. She'd liked being naked in Spain, back here it didn't feel right. The house felt spooked, as if Charmian was there too. Until she'd got rid of Charmian's stuff, it didn't feel like her house. Eric said buy what she liked, make changes. When she had he'd gone berserk. 'What ever happened to Charmian's Sitzendorf?' She didn't know what he meant. He didn't like her nightdresses, she didn't talk right, cook right, dress right. Why should she wear knickers for him? They never made love these days hardly. Most probably Charmian had something to do with it.

Now she couldn't stop shivering, the taxi felt so cold. Why couldn't it snow, instead of this sodding frost? She looked up at the sky through the window, there was Venus looking down. Venus was the goddess of love. Perhaps she should make a wish. Stars were like pictures in the sky. Dead love was worse than hate. She didn't hate him exactly, she just wanted him like he was. Hitting, shouting, swearing in the bedroom. Charmian should have been there tonight. Where was the fine gentleman now? 'Course a teacher doesn't stop teaching once he gets out of school. In Spain he'd been too busy making love to want her to change. Ivy had told her it was easier to go upwards than down, she should study Eric's ways. Why should she? She didn't like his ways, nor understand them. Always going on about taste. He liked awful food himself, things like partridge in wine sauce and caviar. He'd brought a hare home once, with blood coming out of its mouth. Expected her to hang it up, cook it. She'd soon put him right about that. He liked awful cheeses too.

'Okay, Dick?'

You knew where you were with a cat. Simple food, heat and love, they didn't let you down. Why couldn't Eric be ordinary, liking frys, pickled onions, buns? He wouldn't even have a television set. His records and tapes were all plays. He made a fuss about the music she liked. Some people were too posh to live. The room that she loved the best, the bar, he hated most of all. Her musical piano, her tea towels and spouting spittoon were so lovely. Eric must be mad in the head. Good job she had Ivy and Dad. They knew how to enjoy themselves. They ate proper food in a proper home and knew about proper love. Soon be there now, back in Shadwell. Shame really, she had worked so hard. Ivy told her you had to work at marriage. There'd been no love in 'Purple Rest' when she'd got there, there wasn't any there now. Perhaps Charmian had put a curse on it.

'There in a minute, Dick. You'll like the buildings. You'll see.'

Dad might be a bit snappy first, she could always get round him. When he smiled, calling her Vi'let, she felt like flying inside. She'd always liked men with square jaws, not like Eric, all weedy and thin. Eric's long pale cheeks made him sickly. In court, that's where it would end. He could do what he liked then. Take Charmian to his staff parties at school. Charmian could cook hares with blood on them and talk about books and plays. Cruel bitch, calling her 'waif' in that smiling voice. She was jealous of anyone young, worrying about getting ugly, jumping on the scales if she smelled a bun. Them and their cheeses and hares.

'Here I am, Ivy. Home again. At last.'

'I've been ringing and ringing your place, Vee. What ever has gone wrong?'

'Everything. Let me get inside the door.'

'Where's Eric? Oh Vee. Your hair. Oh my lor'.'

'What's wrong with my hair? Don't you like it? Don't laugh, Ivy.'

'It's comic looking. Don't know what Dad will say. It's like a . . . what's inside your coat?'

'My cat, 'course. I wasn't leaving Dick behind.'

'A *cat*? What cat? Where *is* Eric, Vee?'

'I don't know where he is. I don't care either. He went out and left me alone. Hello, Dad.'

'What ever has happened, Vi'let? What ever you done to your hair?'

'I might of known you wouldn't like it. Don't start picking on me. I come in a taxi. It's cold.'

'Your Mum has been worried sick. You didn't say what happened, ringing us so late.'

'I been ringing and ringing, Vee. Got no answer . . .'

She looked at Ivy's pretty face and Dad's brown eyes, all worried looking, and she loved them. They loved her, that was why and she was welcome here. There wasn't a posh bone in either of them, they lived a sensible life, they both had proper-shaped hands.

'Give us a kiss, Dad.'

'Now then, Vee, never mind that. Tell us what's been going on. What's up with you and Eric. Oh my lor', that hair.'

'Stop it, Ivy. I . . . you got a cup of tea?'

'What's that on your neck, Vi'let? Your neck looks all red.'

'Nothing. Leave me alone, Dad. Nothing.'

'Now then, Chester, she's upset. Your neck does look sore though, Vee.'

'Tell you later. You got any whatsits?'

'What do you mean, "whatsits"?'

'Oh you know. I got to change.'

'You come on again have you? (Ches, put the kettle on for Vee.) You're not due are you, Vee?'

'It's not my period, it's Eric. He . . . he went for me.'

'He do that to your neck? It's a bruise. A nasty bruise.'

'Not only that. He . . . put his . . . his hand . . .'

'Oh Christ. Is that all? He never done that before? Don't cry now, lovey.'

'Oh Ivy.'

'There. There.'

She'd never been one for easy crying, she wasn't going to start now. It was Ivy sympathizing that did it. You could put up with things till you got sympathy. Sympathy made you soft. Ivy wouldn't understand. Dad treated her like a queen. She wasn't married to an animal who yelled and did rude things with his hand. Her inside felt sore.

She felt for a piece of gum in her pocket. It was Ivy's fault for making her marry Eric. It was Dad's fault for not stopping her, not putting his foot down. It was Charmian's fault that Eric was so cruel. Didn't anyone understand?

CHAPTER THREE

Ivy

She followed Vee into the bathroom, chewing the inside of her cheek. She had a sore place, she chewed it when she was upset. She didn't want Vee to know she was worried. Poor old Vee, she looked a sight. Imagine her dragging herself over to Shadwell at this time of the night, with her hair sticking out in spikes. And such a colour. Kids today liked playing about with their hair same as they always did, old Vee was the same as the rest, didn't know where to stop. She *had* rushed her into marrying Eric, granted she had. She didn't know he was violent. He and his Mum were so posh, it showed you couldn't tell. He wasn't a Catholic, but then nor was Chester and look how happy they were. She and Ches never rowed. She realized now she'd been too keen to get Vee off their hands into a stranger's arms. He was educated, gentry, a teacher, what more could you ask than that? 'Easier go up than down,' she'd said; now she was not so sure. Vee needed somebody strong, someone to manage her. Vee was spoiled, idle and rude.

Ches hadn't been in favour, had said they ought to wait. 'Don't rush Vi'let,' he'd kept saying, 'now do not rush our girl.' At seventeen she was still more like a ten-year-old. Poor old Vee, no proper youth at all.

She'd wanted her to marry young, not make the mistakes she'd made, that's why she'd been so strict. Too much freedom was a mistake, same as it always was. She'd been lucky with Ches, she granted that. Never looked at anyone else now.

Chester wouldn't stand for it. Besides she was a Catholic, wasn't she? The church knew what was what. She'd not been too particular about Vee's faith, she didn't attend mass herself (Ches not being a believer) but that didn't mean she wasn't a Catholic at heart. She was born one and she'd die one. She believed in a heaven and hell. She had rushed the light of their lives from the school to the altar, now the damage was done. She nibbled her cheek. Poor old Vee was back at the buildings, with tears in her pretty eyes, hair looking like an animal and red marks over her neck. Her hem was coming down too, a bad sign that, she'd been that particular once. 'Purple Rest' wasn't the haven it ought to be, nor Eric the perfect mate. The solution now, as she saw it, was for them to have a child. A kid would settle them. The church said you should stay fresh till you married, and have kiddies after that. You ought to stop together, kiddies helped that, they kept a couple close. Every month since that wedding day she'd waited for some special news. She knew to the minute when Vee should come on. So what was happening now? A grandchild was just what she fancied. Was it bedroom trouble? Could it be Vee was cold?

She still felt choked when she thought of the wedding and Vee in her purple lace with grains of rice scattered over it when she left the church. Ches had said let her wear what she wants, it's her wedding isn't it, not yours. Purple was no colour for a bride. Everything else was a treat. The roses, the candles, the priest's lace vestments. They'd all worn rose button holes. Ches, handing Vee over to Eric, had worn the biggest. He'd begged her not to rush little Vee up to the last. Said it was like trying to get silk from a pig's ear, you couldn't, Vee wasn't Eric's kind. 'What, our Vee a pig? Don't be disgusting,' she'd said to him. Vee could be anything she chose. She'd had the best possible send-off in spite of Eric's mother spoiling it. Charmian, a right countess she was, with her graces and sneers and furs.

Charmian had been the only guest on Eric's side of the

church. A bad sign that, no friends. He couldn't help having no relatives, as Ches pointed out, a man ought to have a friend. Well, it *had* been a small wedding, they had asked few guests themselves. But Charmian left after the promises, too grand to stay for the cake. Her how-now voice hadn't spoken to them, they might as well have all been behind bars. She'd missed the reception, the dance in the parish hall. Ivy had been really upset. She'd danced later with Chester, had made them play their old tune. Later she had cried in his arms to think of Vee far away in Spain, in bed in a stranger's arms. She *had* rushed her, she admitted it, she had done it for the best. Well, she was back now with her hair in tufts and a nasty cat in her arms.

'Your hem is down at the back, Vee.'

'The back? Where? Don't you pick on me too.'

'Is there something you haven't said, something you'd like to say?'

'Like what? What do you mean?'

'I wanted a lovely life for you, you know that, don't you, Vee? I thought Eric would be right.'

She remembered that time when they'd told her that she'd had a baby girl. Such a pretty face, right from the start. Shy-faced, the nurse said, like Mummy, not like the Dad at all. A sweet shy blue-eyed girl. Nurse had rubbed violet powder on her. She'd decided then, call her Violet. A lucky name, Chester thought, he liked it too. He had two flowers in his life. Ivy and Violet. Now here was Vee telling her life wasn't lovely at all, she hated it. Eric was cruel.

'My lord, Vee. What do you mean?'

'It's personal. Filth.'

What did she mean 'filth'? For a man and wife nothing was that. Filth was if you wasn't married. That must be it, Vee was cold.

She'd been such a lovely child; you couldn't help spoiling her. Ches used to load her with toys, she liked playing shop-keepers best. She used to collect ornaments for the shelf in her room. When she'd left to get married the bareness of that shelf seemed to spread right through the flat. They'd missed her pop music too. A blank, a quiet, no Vee. Ivy hadn't ever been one for praying, she believed, though, yes, she did. She'd taken to sitting in Vee's old room, with her transistor, making believe Vee was there. She'd offered little prayers for her that she'd have a nice life with kiddies when she'd grown up a bit. She looked forward to when she would knit for them. Praying made her feel better. Ches worried, kept telling her not to brood. He missed Vee himself, his brown eyes looked so sad. So then she'd started fussing over him. Only right after all. A Catholic wife should put her man first. They were alone again, she'd forgotten how nice that could be. Ches was always a passionate man, three times in a night was nothing. So sex got better and better with no Vee to overhear.

She would do anything Ches wanted her to do, he'd do the same for her. They were that fond of a bit of love. 'Filthy?' Exactly what did Vee mean? Ches did a line in dirty love books at one time, him not being RC. She'd taken a look at them sometimes. You could learn a good deal from a book. She'd done a good job on Vee, keeping her fresh for her wedding. Fresher than cream, she'd been. Could she have overdone that aspect? Could it be Vee was a prude? A man and wife ought to study each other. You had to do right by the children, of course. When they left the nest you had each other again. Leastways it was like that with them. When Vee rang and said she was coming she'd looked over at Ches. She'd sighed. Trouble? Tonight? They didn't want it. It wasn't convenient tonight. Now it looked as if Vee was stopping. Their own girl. Back. Tonight.

Of course they did want her, their little Vee. It was just the unexpectedness. They hadn't expected a cat. She and Ches hated cats. They hated dogs even more. Animal fur didn't suit Chester, particularly fur from a cat. For this reason they'd never kept pets. He got rashes over his arms, fur affected his breathing. They loved to see Vee. That cat was another thing. They missed Vee; they were always talking about her; they didn't want her back. She had Ches to herself again, they had some lovely times, especially at night. Ches was too easy with Vee, she'd have to tell her herself. She could stop here for a night or two, she couldn't stop for good. 'Purple Rest' was her place now. All these stories of fighting and filth were dreadful, granted, but Eric must have had a reason. He'd never hit her for nothing, he was too much of a gent. She felt like hitting Vee herself right now, bothering them with trouble and tears.

'Marriage isn't all roses and promises, there's no need to cry like that.' Vee looked as she used as a child, sitting on the edge of the bath, fists pressed up to her eyes. She'd find a sani-pad right away.

'Tampon. You know I hate those pads.'

'I only got the sanis.'

Age had two sides, good and bad. Those sweats and floods did stop, monthlies did come to an end and sex got best of all. No more fears of any more kids coming, no more being bad-tempered before. Was that Vee's trouble, fear?

She opened the top drawer of the wardrobe. Neat as a picture as always. Ches liked a tidy home, she'd tried to teach Vee the same. She had spent a lot of time improving 'Purple Rest', that she did know, gone to a lot of expense. That house was lovely now, but Vee was untidy too. Ivy judged a home by a neat kitchen and a tidy bed. Untidiness in either of these rooms was a bad sign. Eating and sleeping kept you living, to say nothing of loving in bed. She loved cleaning their bed-room, loved keeping it just so. Putting away his clothes, rolling his socks, ironing his pants was another act of love. Ches liked his side of the bed tucked tightly, liked his pillows built up high. Her nightie went into a red and gold satin heart, his pyjamas folded into a brown plush dog. She loved gold and scarlet, with Christmassy touches of green. She had dyed their nylon fur mats herself in red, yellow and green. She always had

29

flowers in the house. Ches brought home knick-knacks sometimes, or joke lines of his stock that hadn't sold. Vee had a lot of these when she moved to 'Purple Rest'.

She found the pads in her cupboard. She patted her hair, checking it, no sign of grey in her upsweep streaked with gold. She had worn that style since she was a girl. Ches liked it, she'd kept it for him. She couldn't understand Vee making such a fright of herself, all that white powder and dark eyebrows. She'd kept her so lovely as a child, their little princess, nothing was too good, she'd always had the best, had what she'd asked for. She'd been a bit of loner always, never bothered with other kids much. She opened her mouth, peered at her cheek inside, peered at her throat deep down. Oh well.

'Here you are, Vee, lovey. Cheer up. It's not as bad as that.'

Like old times again, in the bathroom, only Vee looked so miserable now. It seemed only yesterday that she'd scrubbed those pink shoulders and rubbed behind those ears. She always cried like a boy, Vee did, always made a lot of noise.

'What did you say, Vee?'

'Eric hates the cat. He hates Dick.'

'He's not the only one. Your father hates them too. I thought you knew.'

'I didn't know. Where is Dick?'

'In the kitchen, most probably. Cats always find where it's warm.'

Vee was a bit selfish, thought the world ran for her benefit. She'd never gone short in her life. New clothes, new shoes, new toys. That trousseau had cost a bomb, all them purply things, she would have them, all purple right through to the bone. Exactly what was the girl up to? Was she planning a kiddy or not? Had she been to a clinic? Seen a doctor? She'd been a virgin bride. Sometimes she felt like stuffing her back into herself, save all this nuisance and gloom. Other times she could strangle her. Was she exaggerating to get attention? She'd always been one for that. Many would give their two eyes to have what she had, a teacher husband, a nice house on that green. Not Vee, oh no, moan, moan.

'Dad never said nothing about not liking cats.'

'He doesn't complain, you know Dad. He has what-sernames – allergies, 'specially from a cat.'

'I've got to stop here, Ivy. There isn't anywhere else. I've got to have Dick.'

'For good, you mean? You can't. It wouldn't be right. Not for good.'

'What are you trying to say, Ivy?'

'You can stop for a bit, for a break, like. There's no need to stop for good. You're married, you're a Catholic wife.'

'Trust you to bring that up when it suits you. It's all rot. I never practised it, nor did you.'

'You was married in church, by a priest. It isn't all rot, it's true. In any case you don't want Eric suing you. You don't want to put yourself in the wrong.'

'Sue? In the wrong? What have I done?'

'The law's a funny thing. You walked out on Eric, don't forget that.'

'I want to leave, I want a divorce. Aren't you and Dad pleased I'm here?'

'Divorce? Never. Not in this family. You can't. You mustn't, Vee.'

'Don't you want me here no more?'

'It isn't that. Cats make Dad ill, I told you. Really ill, the fur.'

It broke her up inside seeing her Vee like this. Nuisance of a girl, sobbing on the toilet again and talking about divorce. She had a loose button as well as that hem and she hadn't really lived. What a purply mess that hair was.

CHAPTER FOUR

Chester

He looked at the cat under the table. It had jumped out of Vi'let's arms to find the warmest place. Its ears were laid flat; cats disliked him as much as he disliked them. For a long time he wouldn't stock cat ornaments or cat pictures, nor even a cat on a towel, he hated them so. It wasn't only his allergy, cats weren't to be trusted, and dogs were even worse. House pets could outsmart you, a lot of animals were cruel. He liked open ways, friendliness. Cats could be choosy too.

He watched the fur on its back ruffling from the heat of the oven. He believed in warm bedrooms and warm kitchens, the most important rooms. Their front room barely got used excepting at Christmas, he didn't like too much heat. Heat made you soft and flabby, that was part of the trouble with Vi'let. The one time he'd visited the corner house on the green he'd felt quite weak with heat. He worried about Vi'let more than he let on. He never wanted her to marry Eric. Ivy had been fooled by his way of life, his job and the words he used. To have their little girl from a 'C' stream click with a teacher was something to be proud of, but marriage was something else. She was only a kid, not a woman, Ivy had rushed her too quick. He'd met too many toffs to be fooled by one; money and a good job didn't make you a good bloke, he'd an idea Eric was a shirker. Vi'let could have got anyone, a good-looking kid like her. He'd been afraid something was wrong when she'd telephoned. When he saw her face he knew. He felt very sorry indeed. Plus now there was this cat, he'd not reckoned on that. Whatever was her bloke thinking about, dispatching his wife across London with her hair looking like that and a cat inside her coat?

'All right, you mog, don't suppose you can help it. Achoo.'

It had already started, first the sneezing, he'd be starting to itch next. His throat and nose were stinging, his eyes felt as if they'd burst. It happened with dogs too and certain sorts of perfume. He wasn't all that bothered with the stuff Violet used, but Ivy's perfume, 'Woodland Whisper', he loved. The first thing he'd noticed about Ivy was the smell of her. He remembered the tune the band had played. 'I Want To Cling To Ivy.' He'd pulled at her hand. 'Dance, darl'?' It seemed so right when she told him her name. They'd hardly been parted since. He'd kept her in 'Woodland Whisper' and whatever else she wished since that night at the *palais de danse*. When Vi'let got born he'd cried, he'd been that happy. He forced himself to lean down now, to touch the cat on the ear.

'What's up with our Vi'let, eh?'

The cat only flicked its ears. They would do what they could for Vi'let, he'd ignore his sneezing and spots. He and Ivy were used to living without her, though they spoke of her every day. What were they up to in the bathroom? What were they talking about? He could hear loud crying.

'You two coming soon, Ivy?'

'In a minute, Ches. We're talking.'

He knew that. What about? The late film was almost finished, they were too busy to bother with him. He and Ivy liked watching the telly, especially before bedtime. He felt unecessary now, he and the cat were kept out. He poured some milk for it, watched it lapping and licking its jaws. It had the fangs of a small alligator and rather an ugly tail. He started to make the tea. When Vi'let had been here he'd not done much in the home. He shared everything with Ivy now. He poured milk into the big jug, skirting the cat by the stove. It lunged at his trouser leg.

'Get away, you cat.'

'What's going on in here, Ches? You get out the biscuits, I'll see to the tea. Or d'you fancy a cocoa, Vee?'

'You know I hate milk. Tea.'

He always liked the table pulled near to the stove, with the telly on the end of it. Once, rather than drink her milk, Vee had poured a mugful into the set. They liked to eat and drink while they viewed. He liked to hear Ivy and Vi'let eating biscuits at the same time as sipping strong tea. Vi'let was still breathing jerkily after all that crying.

The film was almost over. He sighed as he put down his cup. Like old times, the telly, the kitchen smelling of gravy and potatoe pie, and Vi'let. Ivy was a good cook, Vi'let wasn't. She looked pretty, that was enough, he used to tell her, pretty enough to eat. She looked bonier now, her shoulder blades stuck out. Poor old kid seemed poorly as well as that shocking mauve hair. Eric should look after her better, buy her a good telly. You were a freak if you didn't own a set but apparently his lordship put his foot down over it. Lofty ideas could cut you off from life, brains could make you less human. If only he'd stopped that marriage Vi'let wouldn't be sitting there looking so miserable. She used to be such a lively kid, with her pop music and her ideas. 'Purple Rest' was the wrong setting for her and Eric the wrong man. All that central heat and opera music was an unhealthy way of life. The bloke couldn't help his hand, but his world wasn't theirs. You only needed a warm bed and a warm kitchen, the other rooms should stay cool. In his opinion the real difference was their dwellings. This flat in the buildings, where he'd been all his life, was a home and 'Purple Rest' was only a house. Vi'let had done a lot to it, done her best to improve it, she had a long way to go. He'd put up with her perfume, say nothing about her hair, ignore her cat if it would help her. You could see every bump in her backbone, poor old kid, much too thin. He put his hand down to touch

Dick, he felt those teeth again, biting his thumb. He wiped his hand on his handkerchief. They were his two girls, he looked after them, he had a lot to be grateful for. The boy and girl in the musical sang into each other's faces before their final kiss. Ivy and Violet looked like twins, blinking, looking enraptured. They didn't make films like that any more, Ivy said. Vi'let sucked a piece of her hair.

'Where is the cat to sleep, Vi'let? I'll find a box if you like.'

'He'll sleep along with me 'course. Same as he always does.'

'That's dirty, Vi'let.'

He swallowed. What she did with her husband in that house on the green was one thing; did she have to do the same here? She probably had a lot to put up with, Eric being the lordly bloke he was. But he had problems too. Cats in the bed weren't right, particularly that cat. Look at her now, kissing its ears. Bits fell from its fur, it dribbled when it purred, it scratched. He wouldn't say anything himself, leave Ivy to speak later on. Its mouth was making Vi'let's hair wet. She came running back home when it suited her, expecting to have her own way. Perhaps she'd leave after she'd had a rest.

'You needn't look like that, Dad. He's my cat, he stops with me.'

'Some things aren't suitable, Vi'let. You aren't a child now, the cat is fully grown. What about its food?'

'He takes what I take. He likes meals on the table by me.'

He was relieved to hear Ivy say that if the cat went on her table, it wouldn't know what had hit it. His Vi'let. Flaming 'eck, where did she get her ideas? She took no notice of either of them, went on kissing the cat's tail. He wondered if she treated Eric as lovingly; she was young in more ways than one. Possibly Eric pestered her too often, some girls didn't like it night after night. Still, she was Ivy's daughter, they were probably both alike. He'd heard her ask Ivy for a sanitary towel. She probably needed to sleep. He felt more sympathy towards Eric; a cat in the bed must be as bad as a cold wife. He oughtn't to have called Vi'let unclean.

Early in the morning he had a bad dream, waking up in a sweat. They'd been at the seaside, he'd been there, yet not there, had heard her calling. He heard tears in her voice, couldn't find her. Ivy? Ivy? He woke up saying her name. He touched her hair, there she was, deeply sleeping as always. Ivy never had dreams, a sign of a good conscience, they said. She hadn't told him yet about Vi'let's trouble, had fallen asleep without even kissing him, she'd been that exhausted, so he still felt left out in the cold.

He got up early to make the morning tea. Ivy liked her first sip before even opening her eyes. He liked watching her eyes waking, so innocent, a purplish blue. Vi'let had the same coloured eyes, with lashes she covered in black. Ivy never looked ugly, in bed or out of it, even in curlers and grease.

At first, when Vi'let left home, she went quiet, shutting herself away in Vi'let's room, listening to her tranny, and, he suspected, praying a bit. Religion never interfered in their married life. Ivy might talk a lot, she didn't bother with mass. There'd been no question of more children either, he took care of that himself. Ivy worried him when she went so quiet, so he'd started to fuss over her more. He started the early tea habit and showed extra love in bed. She liked eating nougat and surprise packets of crisps. He brought home flowering plants and got in as early as he could. He felt nothing he did was too good for her, a good job they'd only one child. Vi'let was special, they missed her, they loved being on their own.

He turned the oven up high. He took the milk in from the step, being careful to make no noise. The bottle tops were rimmed with frost. He blew on his fingers. He wasn't like everyone else, wasting good money on heat; paraffin heaters and fires were an extravagance. The oven was better than anything, you got a good heat quick. The fug was soon as good as last night. The cheapest was often the best. Now, Ivy's tea.

'Here you are, Ive. Three sugars, top of the milk, stirred.'

'What time is it?'

'Not six o'clock.'

'Vee might like a tea. She might wake up feeling strange. She isn't well, you know.'

'I know she isn't. She's too thin, poor old kid. What's wrong?'

'She ran away from her house, she's scared.'

'She ran away from Eric. It's his house too. Why?'

'I'm worried, Ches.'

'She left him for good?'

'She can't, she's a Catholic. Besides . . .'

'What?'

'We spoiled that girl, Ches.'

'I know. What did happen last night at the house?'

'He hit her. Went for her. I mean, they row, they've not had a hitter before.'

'But . . .the . . . I'll do for him.'

He felt helpless again, and left out. Why hadn't Vi'let told him, didn't she trust him or what? He watched Ivy sip her tea, watched her reach for her dressing-gown; she must see if Vee was awake. She didn't shut the girl's door after her, he could see Vi'let's sleeping head. She was lying on her stomach, the way she always did, with one hand under her cheek, that coloured hair was all over the place, her sleeping face was white. Her body made a long thin mound under the cover, with a smaller mound behind. He might have guessed that dirty cat would be near. He'd forgotten how long her lashes were, when she rubbed they were like insect legs. Such blue eyes, he couldn't stop watching. Flaming 'eck, he was her father, why couldn't he watch if he wanted, why couldn't he go in the room? The smaller mound started moving up the bed.

'What ever time is it, Ivy? You know I hate being woken early.'

'You aren't at "Purple Rest" now, miss. Your Dad's made a

pot of tea.'

Ivy sounded quite sharp again. The cat poked its nose through Vi'let's hair. It had the same bad look in its eyes.

'You had that great animal with you all night, Vee? Don't be so dirty.'

'I told you, Ivy, Dick sleeps here. Now you've woken us both.'

He hated to think of his daughter making a fool of herself over a cat. He heard Ivy explaining that they couldn't be doing with a cat in this home, she'd already told her that.

'Okay, I get your point. You're telling me I must go. I'm not wanted, right.'

'Don't be so hasty. I never said that.'

'It's what you meant, though. Well I'm not going back to Eric again, you needn't think I am.'

'Vee, don't be like that now. Ches, tell Vee she can stay.'

It was good to be included, needed, a part of them again. He said that he would start the breakfast. He liked to get out early. He was due at Slough market this morning, he'd eat a good fry-up first, as well as having sandwiches for eating later on. Vee used to enjoy her breakfast, especially sausage and egg.

'What, me? Breakfast? Ugh.'

'No wonder you're so boney and white.'

He couldn't bear to think of her and Eric having hitters. The girl must stay here, that was clear. That clicky family she'd married into weren't all they seemed.

'Cheese, Chester? Or Marmite? I'll cut two double rounds.'

He'd take both, and some of the sugar biscuits if any were left from last night. Nobody made sandwiches like Ivy. He liked watching her work, she was so cheerful. She sang nicely and had such refinement. How or where Vi'let got her ideas he couldn't think, with her purple notions and lip. You'd travel far to find a lovelier girl, though; couldn't Eric realize that? 'Course Vi'let could be enlarging the whole thing. Why hadn't she hit him back? Eric might be a teacher, he was also quite a weed, plus there was that handicapped hand, surely she could put up some kind of a show? He felt pushed into a false position. The girl ought to go back, face things. She was an embarrassment here. He wanted her to stay.

'Come on, Ches, don't look so miserable. Switch the radio on.'

'I want to cling to Ivy, if Ivy will cling to me.' Their song playing, the song they'd heard when they'd met. He loved her even more now, if possible, his loving and sexy wife.

'Get off, Ches, don't start that, not in front of Vee. Here's your plate.'

She smelled so nice, so did his breakfast. His sausage had burst in the pan.

'Come along, Vee, lovey. Have a sausage?'

'Oh get away.'

'Vi'let, you shouldn't talk to Ivy like that. Whatever is wrong?'

'Leave her. She's tired, Ches.'

'I'm not. Stop telling me what I am. What I ought to do. I'm fed up.'

'Have a slice of toast?'

'I've said no. What's the matter with you two? You keep picking on me. Stuffing me with food.'

He didn't answer. His egg was perfectly fried, the yolk filmed over with white. Well basted, that's what he liked. He put a piece of fried bread from his plate on to Vi'let's, like he used to when she was a kid. He gave her half his egg, buttered some toast for her. Her hair was lovely and silky still under that colour she used.

'Let her do that herself, Ches.'

He said that she needed tempting and feeding up. He took his sandwiches, wrapped in a plastic bag, took his thermos from Ivy.

'Well, I'm off now, darl'.'

He loved her hands touching him when she settled his

woollen scarf, loved that last sniff of 'Woodland Whisper'. He'd try to put up with the cat.

'Suppose you'll be here tonight, Vi'let? You're still our girl, you know.'

'Suppose I will. I'll stop here if Dick can.'

He hadn't driven the van to the end of the street when he heard Ivy calling. Vi'let was on the kitchen floor, crying and screaming with pain.

CHAPTER FIVE

Eric

She'd be with that family of hers in Shadwell, he had no doubt about that. She was still tied to her mother, the umbilical cord still held strong. She was weak-kneed, she was unstable, worst of all she had no friends. He ought to have been forewarned. People without friends had a character defect. No doubt at this moment she was complaining about him to her mother, if she wasn't glued to the television screen. Violet had left *him*, he must remember that, it could be important. At the same time he must remember to be magnanimous, he was a middle-class professional, a person of some standing, though the appearance of the house belied that, thanks to Violet's efforts. Leniency had achieved nothing, she was actually getting worse. *She* had provoked the scene in the bedroom; his conscience was quite clear. He had cared for her like a lap-dog, let her do what she chose. She'd never had to earn her living – the petted darling of the house. He'd abandoned all hope of improving her. If she'd show a glimmer of interest in him or his work he'd be satisfied, but she didn't and never had. Considering he worked at her old school you might imagine she'd care a little. She had no notion of loyalty. The truth was he felt ashamed of her. It was the more tragic that she could have been educable were it not for her background. Low life had rotted her mind.

She'd gone sneaking off to those parents, no goodbye, no message for him. Her family had much to answer for, the self-indulgent pup. Well, they were welcome to her. She'd come back when she got bored. She'd miss the comfort he offered as well as his cash. She obviously thought his funds were limitless the way she spent, or left money around in purses and bags. The rooms he provided were spacious, that Peabody flat was cramped. He sighed. He'd totally failed to change her, on the contrary she had changed him. He couldn't look anywhere without seeing purple trash and vulgarity. When she did return he would forgive her, naturally; she was after all still his wife. His wife and his love. What had happened to them since they'd left Spain? He thought of those eyes again looking at him. 'You animal, you should be on four legs.' What kind of logic had she under that lovely face?

Outside on the green he'd felt furious. He was better now, quite calm. He'd keep his equilibrium, tension was weakening. He walked about downstairs, observing. Plaster and plastic objects, so dear to her childish heart, useless ashtrays, coloured insects, monstrously shaped and sized. He went into the bedroom again. He looked closely at the dark specks on the puce-coloured sheets. He might have guessed; cat fleas. It probably had lice as well, and worms. Cats spread their infections as well as their filthy dirt. He stripped the sheets off, folding them. His clothes felt uncomfortable now. He would find a clean shirt and fresh sheets. Dealing with the laundry was another of Violet's weak points; she never planned ahead though he'd provided every electrical aid. As he had feared the airing cupboard was empty apart from the cat's pillow. The laundry hamper was crammed. What was the use of that expensive washing machine; there was nothing clean to be found. He needed another bath. He would lie down then, try and rest before setting off for school. How agreeable to have the bed to himself, to move without touching a cat, to lie without being eaten by fleas, or choking on that scent.

He stretched out in unscented water. He liked bathing without being interrupted. Violet's habit of entering without knocking was offensive, though he had loved it once. She didn't understand shyness, didn't know what reticence was. He was always aware of his hand, he felt at his worst without clothes. He didn't like her sitting on the toilet when he was in the bath; to make it worse the cat followed her everywhere. He hated its staring eyes and unpleasant snarling mouth.

He lay on top of the eiderdown in his pyjamas. He couldn't relax, he felt stifled, his heart was beating much too fast. He'd go down and have a whisky. He rarely drank, he applauded moderation, especially in food and drink. Besides that, his whisky was in the old dining-room which Violet had changed into a bar. She'd made it uninhabitable with her joke spittoon, her piano and musical cigar boxes. He made himself go in again. The smell was thickest here. He'd not been inside since Christmas, which they had spent alone, unhappily. On Boxing Day she'd gone over to Shadwell to her parents. Paper chains and holly still hung from the chandelier. There was the mistletoe under which no one had kissed. The bar, shaped like a mock beer barrel, was stacked with fizzy drinks, Fanta, Seven-Up and Babycham and bottles of cherryade. Where was the tantalus with the beautiful decanters, Charmian's wedding gift? He'd asked Violet to take particular care of that, he had filled the decanters himself. The brandy, port, whisky and sherry were locked and ready in the tantalus, waiting for when they had guests. He had the key, he reached for it. The lock of the tantalus was broken, the silver labels ripped from their chains. Three glass stoppers lay on the floor, the trash bucket was full of glass. The whisky decanter was on the sill with a union jack in it and a used joss stick. Violet wasn't only a vandal, she must be out of her mind. The sole of his shoe stuck to a lollipop paper. He went out and closed the door.

The kitchen was stifling, the heat monitor was on full. For the sake of his school work he must rest. He'd drink some coffee if he could find any. There wasn't any milk. The cat's needs came before his. In the fridge were tins of salmon and a packet of sugar buns. He longed to smell coffee freshly ground, he even longed for a cigarette though he'd not smoked for several years.

He got a pencil and sat at the table. He would jot down a few ideas for his play about family love. The BBC had stipulated that the entries must be previously unpublished and the work of a non-professional writer. The closing date for submission was 1 August of this year. He was determined to enter and win. Time was his main hindrance, he was scarcely ever alone, writing demanded solitude. There was no privacy at school and Violet was always at home. She was so noisy. He longed to listen to something of his on the radio. If this happened he'd never feel lonely, nor would he ever complain. His marriage was a disaster, he hated teaching English literature, he wanted to write plays. Drama fascinated him, this play was his second chance. Why had she broken the decanters? How could he forgive her? My wife, my love, come back.

He started worrying over his opening speech, he didn't hear the postman at the gate. He heard a letter being pushed through the flap, he saw the American stamp. He opened it, his eyes blurred. 'The Admissions Board of the Writing Centre has examined your case and is pleased to offer you a place here for the month of March. If you are still interested could you let us know and we will let you have further details.'

It was mid-February now. He'd forgotten about the Centre, he'd applied months ago, in answer to an advertisement in a literary magazine. Occasional places were offered to non-residents of the States, with expenses partly paid. He had filled in the form on a whim, not expected to hear any more. He'd told Charmian, but nobody else. Violet didn't know even that he had ambitions to write.

In his college days his sketches had received high praise. The *Radio Times* sponsored the play competition; so far he'd made scant progress. His plan to use the dining-room as a study came to nought, thanks to Violet who had made it a bar. He was alone now for the first time since Boxing Day. He hadn't felt so clear-headed for years. This letter gave him hope. He re-read it. A brochure was enclosed with a picture of the Centre, a fine building with white steps leading to a porch. Around it were woods of tall trees. Another picture showed a group of American writers, presenting contented smiles. He would be one of them, a writer, for the whole of the month of March, his expenses partly paid. He had to pay something – rather a large amount actually – but their standard of living was high, he had no objections. No more aloneness for him, the cream of the American literary world would be his companions.

He had never travelled as far; the change, the adventure would be just what he needed. Easter was late this year. The school closed for three weeks, he would take one week off from work. This letter in his left hand was a lifeline. How fortunate that he'd never told Violet about it, the less she knew the better. Let her think his trip was connected with school. She might ask to come with him otherwise.

He was tired of being ashamed of her, he yearned for acceptance among people of discernment and sensitivity. She could remain in Shadwell, or return here when he'd gone. This was a gift from the heavens; he aspired, he would succeed. He would finish 'Family Loves', submit it when he returned. Violet would be proud of him, she'd never despise him again.

He was in no mood for whisky now, he felt ravenous. He opened one of the tins of pink salmon, eating from it with a fork – something that Violet might do. This morning he didn't care, he'd let standards slide. He could even think more kindly about her decanter-breaking; poor girl, she didn't understand. The longer he looked at the letter the happier he felt. He, an English writer, amongst that privileged band. He must be rational, he mustn't delude himself, this invitation didn't ensure success, he was storming a formidable citadel, you needed luck as well as merit, especially with radio plays. If he failed it would not be through lack of endeavour, he had the determination, he hoped he had the skill. He had sent the Centre one of the sketches from his early student days. He thought he had broadened spiritually as well as artistically since those days. The character of a writer was as important as his skill, hard work mattered a lot. He didn't want to teach English for the rest of his working life. The school, with so many students like Violet or worse, depressed him. He needed a regular salary to keep her in purple trash and even if they did separate he would still have to maintain her, in Shadwell or wherever she chose. The cat episode proved, if proof were needed, how dissimilar they were. New England sounded refreshing, with a beautiful climate in spring.

When the telephone rang he hoped it might be Charmian.

'Hello? Oh. Ivy. How are you?'

'How am I? It's not me I'm concerned about. It's Vee.'

'Oh really? What's wrong with her? What about her? I'm just about to leave for school.'

'Well, school can wait, Eric. I'm not a person to interfere between a man and wife. Marriage is holy, we know that. But what has been going on?'

'I beg your pardon? Going on?'

Why should he defend himself? Why be humble? He'd done nothing. 'Remember you're a Caive-Propp,' Charmian used to say. He needn't fear anyone called Stubbs.

'It's Vee's pardon you should be begging. You ought to be on your knees. I'm warning you, Eric, you could be finding yourself in court.'

'Court? What court?'

He'd be late at school, he wanted to talk to the Head about taking a week from teaching.

'Police court. Wake up, it's not a trifle if what Vee says is true. Is it true?'

'I have no inkling what she's said. Violet can be imaginative when she wants to be. Please, I am going to be late.'

'Don't make out to be so innocent. You hurt my girl. You

mistreated her.'

'I didn't, I assure. Not purposely.'

'Not purposely? You hurt her badly. She fainted early this morning. The doctor has just left.'

'Doctor? Is there something wrong with Violet? Please let me speak to her.'

'She's not to move, not to get up. She's been told she must rest.'

'Please, Ivy, what has Violet said? She's not really ill, is she?'

'You done a mischief. Common assault. Complete rest, no worry, the doctor said.'

'But what is it?'

'It's early to tell yet. She could be pregnant. More than likely, he said.'

'A child? Violet? She's . . . oh . . .'

'She may not be now, thanks to you. You animal, hurting her, packing her off.'

'I had no idea, Ivy. This is tremendous news. We . . . didn't . . . we . . . wanted . . . Tremendous . . . But . . .'

'But nothing. You could find yourself in court.'

'We . . . I couldn't divorce her if what you say is true.'

'I'm talking about Vee. She might sue you.'

'But her church, Ivy. You can't surely mean that?'

'My poor little daughter. She's suffered.'

'I assure you I was actuated. The provocation was extreme. She keeps her cat in our bed, did you know that? And other things, besides.'

'I know. I do know. I don't approve, nor does Ches. But she's your wife and it's your cat. You were brutal.'

'I tried, Ivy. Really I did.'

'Not enough. Not nearly enough. If anything happens to her, if she loses it, you're the one to blame.'

'I can't believe this has happened. May I telephone later?'

He mustn't allow her to gain ascendancy. Her bombastic attitude was absurd. But . . . a baby? Violet's and his?

Unbelievable.

Nothing in the world must stand in the way of his American trip. The news couldn't have come at a more inconvenient time. He found a tea-bag in a broken cup. He sipped strong black tea and considered. Ivy's voice rang in his ears. 'Your wife and your cat. Brutal.'

He tidied the sink, he washed everything, including the cat's mauve dish. There was fur over everything. He got a dustpan and stiff brush, fur clung so, the carpets, the curtains, the chairs. 'You done a mischief. Common assault.' He was trembling, he wouldn't go into the bar again, he might not be able to control himself. He wanted to run amok with an axe. His decanters. Common assault.

He must tell Charmian. Not about the child of course, not yet, it wasn't certain. It could be a false alarm. But his trip to America was definite. She'd be as excited as he. As he dialled he pictured her moving towards her telephone, unhurriedly stretching her hand.

'Charmian. Listen. I have good news.'

He pictured her smile of delight. She was so disciplined, so loving, so right. Compared with his mother Ivy Stubbs was simply another species, though they both had mothered a child.

'Darling.'

Such warmth, such intonation, the 'r' delicately stressed. Her hair, her face, her clothes were always immaculate, whatever the time of day. She had never shown the pain that she must have felt over his marriage, apart from that one warning when he'd been too paralysed with love to listen. She had been right, of course. And yet . . . had she been right? He felt so confused. How much did Violet need him at this juncture? Which needed his attention the most, his play or his possible child? Both of them incurred gestation, both resulted in birth. But the play was a certainty, her pregnancy was not. She might abort, she might be mistaken, this invitation to the

States was a fact. Art – literature in particular – was vitally important, anyone could have a child. Charmian would agree with him, no need to bother her with problems apart from his coming trip.

'Er . . . Would you like to keep an eye on this place for the month of March? I'm going to have to be away.'

'Away? And taking the little waif too?'

He had never objected to her habit of referring to Violet as 'waif'. Sometimes she called her 'mopsy' in her lightly smiling tone. Violet was rather waif-like sometimes, or a mopsy who'd fallen from grace. 'You done a mischief . . . common assault . . . pregnant.' What a hideous voice Ivy had.

'Oh . . . we had a slight altercation. Nothing serious, nothing drastic. *Mea culpa*, I must admit.'

She never probed. How he appreciated her, that was all he need say at this point. If his present plan succeeded he'd return a playwright as well as a father to be. Charmian's tone was dry as she remarked that the waif, if she was staying behind, might not be overjoyed to see her.

'Oh she's with her mother at the moment. In Shadwell, she needn't find out. If you could just look in on this house from time to time.'

'Of course. I remember. Shadwell. Poor pet, when did all this happen? When did the waif abscond?'

'Last night.'

'You sound absolutely exhausted, my pet.'

'I am. You see, Charmian, I've just heard from the States, from that Writers' Centre I applied to, do you remember? I'm accepted. I'm going there to finish my play.'

'Wonderful. I'm overjoyed. I'll come to your rescue. Have no fear, if the waif has run off I'll hold your little fort. You can rely on me.'

'She hasn't run away, she's visiting her mother, I told you. In Shadwell. If you could just keep an eye on the house.'

She told him not to give the matter another thought, he

knew she wouldn't fail him. She explained that under no circumstances would she sleep in the house, she couldn't, not after what the waif had done to it, her aura no longer fitted there. But she'd come over, keep the place aired, take in any letters.

'The house must be kept warm. In case Violet wants to come back . . . I mean she won't come back, not for a while. She can't at the moment . . . She might come I suppose, if she . . . nothing is arranged.'

He ought to tell Charmian about the baby, he must tell her. Not just now.

'You sound a trifle confused, my sweet. Have no fear, I'll do everything I can.'

'Goodbye then, Charmian. I must get off to school.'

CHAPTER SIX

Charmian

She fingered her seed pearls. She liked wearing them regularly. Usage improved pearls. Beautiful things, clothes, jewels or furniture should be displayed and used. Her triple twist of pearls, newly cleaned and strung, were particular favourites. She'd had a premonition when she awoke this morning that she might hear good news. She had been right. She tapped her shoe, watching the light reflected in the leather. She never wore slippers except from her bath to her bed. Slippers were bad for the arches as well as slovenly. Her silky blouse was fresh, her cardigan newly cleaned. It wasn't nine o'clock yet but standards mattered. Good clothes, orderly habits mattered. Anything cheap or imitative offended her. The good news had come over the telephone. She had received it properly dressed. She glanced into her cheval-glass. The pearls, slightly warm now, picked up her skin tones so well. She regretted that she had no daughter to inherit her jewellery. The thought of the waif touching anything of hers was disagreeable, particularly her pearls. She would rather the name of Caive-Propp died than have the line vitiated by bad blood. This possibility would be removed if the waif and Eric split up. He had sounded quite overwrought. She could understand his agony of mind; the girl had a sensual charm and her boy was loyal. He would recover. She could only pray that the rift would be a permanent one, that no issue of theirs would ever tarnish the family escutcheon. Let the waif stay in Shadwell for good.

She felt elated, a trembling, a loss of control. She set store by control, over herself and over other people. Inadequate people needed to be controlled by the adequate. She never preached, the less you pontificated the greater your control. She tried never to worry. Worry weakened the worrier. So, the waif had abandoned Eric. This was a jubilee day. His news from the States, his little literary project would occupy his mind, heal his wounded pride. It scarcely mattered if the project succeeded or failed. The prayed-for rift had come earlier than she had dared hope; her jewels and pearls would be safe. Soon Eric would be free.

She tapped her shoe, she tried to lengthen her breathing inhalation. In . . . out . . . peace. She took up her embroidery and threaded her needle with green. So many leaves to be filled before she had earned a strawberry to outline and colour with red. She dipped her needle in and out, finishing off her leaf. Now for the scarlet, her reward. By the time the strawberry was completed her pulse-beat was normal again. She gathered up her silks, folding the linen away. Some people prayed, she sewed. She loved tapestry; her chair covers would take a long time. She spent less time in her antique gallery since Eric had married and left. She never became bored. Her doctor insisted that she took more rest because of her heart. She wasn't as strong now. So she got up later, only opened her gallery on three afternoons a week. Her customers had been dealing with her for years; the aristocracy were loyal, they spent freely, they told their friends. She'd never advertised. Every morning she kept her simple account books, wrote to her clients, made her little flat charming. She ran her small business alone, apart from old Truss, an odd-job man who helped with the heavier work. When stocks were low he sometimes went knocking on doors for her. She had taught Truss what to look for, how to drive a bargain.

She was fond of her flat, fond of improving it. Her present

kitchen would have fitted into the pantry of her old home, her bathroom was cupboard-sized. It had been a shock when Eric had bought his house on the green and moved out. He had produced his waif and left. She had not shown her feelings, she had simply sold up the old home and moved here, having given Eric the pick of her furniture. Life changed, became quieter. He'd been her world, he had left. She never complained. He'd taken her love and her strength, but that was a mother's lot. He must use his own judgement with regard to his choice of a wife. She disliked self-pity. He had his own future, in teaching or the writing of plays, she had done all she could for him. By spending less time in her gallery she had more time for her home. Her husband had died before Eric's birth. When he left her for the waif it felt like another death. She had smiled though she'd cried inside. Above all she never complained. With her small new flat and her gallery just three times a week she had more time to herself. Of course Eric needed his own house. Of course he needed a wife. She held her chin high, though at times her smile felt tight.

The first time she had seen the waif it was like poison thrown in her face. She had greeted her with punctilio. 'So you are Miss Stubbs. Eric has spoken so warmly of you.' She'd tried not to blink at the girl's reply. 'Warmly? Suppose he has, seeing we're getting hitched. Soon I'll be Violet Caive-Propp.' And she'd opened those eyes and grinned. Those unnatural lashes were worse than a cartoon, she was totally without grace. Charmian wished that she was Lady Caive-Propp, though it probably wouldn't help. The girl obviously didn't know the meaning of deference. She had smiled her best smile. 'A wedding? When? Wonderful.' She had asked her how long she had left school, if she had a job. Had Eric taught her? She had listened to the reply. 'What me? I don't fancy work, I left school at sixteen.' Charmian had given Eric her warning then. 'If you marry that girl you will rue it. You'll be alone, you'll be lonely. I have never known it work, the differences are too pronounced. You must of course use your own judgement.' Of course he wouldn't be swayed. So be it. She had smiled. Her new home claimed her attention, she never was idle. Since her practitioner's warning she indulged herself each morning with early tea in bed, not breakfast of course, but a half cup of weak china tea, leaning back on her pillows before taking her morning bath. Wisdom didn't necessarily stem from experience but from keeping your self-control.

She didn't reproach herself about Eric's lack of friends. He was a sensitive, had never been part of a group, nor shown interest in the opposite sex until he'd met that waif. They neither had needed anyone, they'd been content together in the perfect bond, a mother and her son. He'd been caught by the first cheap face, was lost to her.

She regarded sexual promiscuity with abhorrence. Sex before marriage was messy. Self-indulgence was as bad as lowered standards. The waif had no social background, no education, no *savoir faire*, her cultural tastes didn't extend further than the cheapest television soap operas, she was a Catholic and wore appalling clothes. She felt glad that her husband was dead, hadn't lived to see his son's error. Their own marriage had been satisfactory, no class conflict, no messiness, no doubts. She had managed the home, cooked beautifully, given way to her husband's wishes in all things. Provided she lost no sleep, of course. The one time he had omitted to 'cover himself' her Eric had been conceived. She hadn't complained. Eric was her lifeline after her husband died. When he was born, half sitting, half lying in bed she had seen his hand before they told her about it, seen the crumpled arm with the thumb set in the wrist, seen the one finger pointing as if to accuse. 'Minor blemish', 'slight malformation', 'nothing serious', they had murmured, breaking it gently, too late. She didn't allow the pain of self-reproach to replace the pain of birth. The pills she had swallowed after her husband died might or might not account for the disfigurement. So be it. No tears, no regrets. What others might regard as a curse she had turned into a blessing. She became father and friend as well as mother to her left-handed son until the waif spoiled everything. She had never swallowed a pill of any kind since his birth. She had adjusted to the situation. Background, heritage mattered, like should marry like. Some people (the waif was one of these) were simply inferior. It was to be hoped they'd not have a child. This news that she'd just received might be the reprieve, a second chance for her boy.

She had stayed aloof from the wedding plans, hoping until the last that the whole poisonous notion would fall through. She'd not suggested another meeting with the waif, she'd put her out of her mind. She tried to believe that she'd imagined her, that Eric hadn't produced her for inspection, his left hand holding her right. Eric had been nervous, had stayed nervous for the months preceding the wedding. As for Charmian, she had risen to the occasion. When she saw Eric wouldn't be dissuaded, she'd made plans to move to this flat. She had donated her best antiques.

On the day she had donned her seed pearls, put on muted silks, purposely playing down her entrance. It was, after all, the bride and bridegroom's day. With her dark frock, her dark sable cloak and toque blending with the pew, she knelt, pretending to pray. Behind her closed eyes she mentally gathered strength. With the exception of her chauffeur, old Truss at the back of the church, there were – thankfully – no other guests on the bridegroom's side, no one to pity her shame. She looked round the garish church. Papist art, as she'd expected, scrolls and painted curlicues, statuary and mystery. She disliked the lurking undertones of the incense that suggested something less pleasant, a smell of the working class. It wasn't necessarily dirt, but a thickness that suggested stupidity and ignorance, plus a refusal to recognize worth.

There, the other side of the aisle, was her son's new family.

That woman wearing the fearsome corsage and the tight shoes, mopping her eyes, was his new mother-in-law. That man in the bright brown suit, also near to tears, was his father-in-law, leading the waif up the aisle. A junk vendor by trade, with a barrow of knick-knacks, the sort that used to be called a spiv. He was the least repellent, with his weathered face, greased curls and loudly squeaking shoes. He had large knuckled hands and rather a kindly face. By the altar rail stood her son, his right hand in his pocket, with eyes for no one but the waif, looking evil in purple lace. She had listened to vows being uttered, her Eric's pure tones, the waif's cockney whine. She left the church. Enough was enough. She'd had no qualms about leaving, had she stayed longer, for the photographs, the kissing and wine, she might have broken and let herself down. These people couldn't help themselves, salt of the earth they might be, they had no social flair. No one noticed her departure, they were too overcome with tears. Weddings encourage facile emotions, especially amongst the vulgar herd. What hurt her most was that Eric didn't notice, he didn't smile when she entered, didn't mention her absence later at the wedding breakfast.

Back in her small bathroom she had cried. She had pictured him posing for the photographer, with that grinning girl on his arm. She had pictured him cutting the cake, his left hand over her right and she'd cried again. He would drink with her, kiss her later, his eyes never leaving her. He should have mixed more with the daughters of her friends. What friends? She only had clients. His expression at the altar had been lewd, predatory. He ought to have mixed with more girls.

She had patted her cheeks, fluffed her hair. She wouldn't think about the bride's purple-laced body being touched by Eric, she wouldn't think about the lace being removed. The waif wore the ring now. They were both Mrs Caive-Propp. She had acted correctly, been generous, she had furnished that house on the green.

After she had consulted her practitioner about her giddiness she had begun her chair-covers and waited for the couple to return from Spain. He had sounded tired when he did telephone, his voice lacked his usual concern. In sweet tones she'd asked after the waif, her daughter-in-law now, the first lady in his life. Eric of course had been hoping to change her, she could have told him that the waif was a lost cause, only death could remould her. With a slight reluctance in his voice Eric had invited her to visit them in the house on the green. She knew her duty, she couldn't refuse one visit, the marriage was finalized now.

She would never forget that warm autumn day. Leaves fell on to the bonnet of old Truss's car, red brown gusts of them. It was dusty. The holly berries forecast a hard winter. When she saw the gate of the house painted in that crude shade she guessed that there would be further shocks.

Old Truss had stayed in the car, she had gone inside alone. She still disliked thinking about it. All her beautiful things, where were they? Her Worcester figurines? Her Sitzendorf? Her Persian rugs? Her Chippendale was gone; where was the davenport? Was there nothing beautiful left? There was ugliness everywhere, cheap upholstery, steel tubing, mock fur. The amount and strength of purple colouring hurt her eyes. She had blinked and kept her smile. The waif, with pride and confidence, had thrown open the door of the dining-room, where Eric intended to work. Beer barrels, graffiti, brass cannon, soda pop. Did they plan to open a pub? No sign anywhere of her Victorian watercolours. Cotton tea towels hung in their place. 'How . . . quaint. Do you entertain much?' she had asked with heroic calm. She saw Eric's shamed expression, she didn't probe any further, didn't search for her tantalus. The house was a mockery of plastic flowers, animals and jokes. The waif was truly poisonous, her effect on the house most grave. She had then willed that the two would split up as soon as possible. She had drunk instant coffee from a thick mauve mug, had looked at the waif silently. 'You will fail here, you will leave this house on the green.'

Now it had happened, the spell had worked. With the waif on her way out, Eric could start to live again. She would do all in her power to remove all taint of her while he was away in the States. When her traces were gone Eric would need her, rely on her as he once had.

She got up quickly, started pacing the room. She sat down. 'Take it easy,' her practitioner had warned. Her chest hurt, the excitement, her eyes burned in her face. She wasn't malicious, she'd never wished anyone ill, nothing serious, never illness or death. Their union had been doomed anyway. They'd be much happier apart.

CHAPTER SEVEN

Charmian

One of her rare extravagances was travelling by cab. Old Truss was almost eighty, she didn't wish to impose on him. Besides, she didn't feel as safe now, with him behind the wheel. She had no more time now to lie back on her starched pillows, considering her tired heart. She had work to do. The corner house on the green waited to be saved. She felt almost proprietorial. That house needed her. It was as simple as that.

She had waved Eric off to the States, from the busy airport. She'd worn her fur toque again. She had watched him walk to the reception lounge, his passport in his left hand. Her own left hand held the prize, the key to his front door. The smaller key for the inner door was in her purse. She'd gone straight there from the airport, travelling by cab, to start putting right the wrong.

She had closed her gallery for the time being, told old Truss to rest.

Her first task had been the gate, replacing the numerals. Names and first impressions mattered. She felt rejuvenated, she was in harness, she was caring for Eric again, her hands and heart working as one.

After a week she felt she'd been there for years, there was so much to do. She had no extra rest now, no time to think of herself. She had started sleeping there, to save time in travelling. She didn't view it as work, though, more a holiday. She was restoring and replenishing Eric's and her world.

She checked each room carefully, not flinching, making lists. The only things Violet hadn't got her claws into were Eric's papers and books. She touched them thoughtfully, one of these days she would read them herself. It was doubtful if the waif read anything above the level of a comic book. She took down the crawling purple curtains, replacing with cream and grey silk. She contacted a decorator. The guns, the spittoon, the fruit machine and fake piano were piled on to a totter's cart. They would most likely end in some fairground, giving pleasure to other plebs. Violet's bar would soon be fit to dine in again, or for studying Eric's works. He had told her to make any changes she thought fit, he wanted a habitable home. All that plastic and purple, out with it, reinstate good taste. He had waved his strange-shaped hand as he used to when he'd left for school. This parting was different. Anticipation, not tears. A writer of plays needed a properly appointed house to work in. She hadn't seen any of his work; it was doubtless brilliant. He needed a woman's help. The waif, with her animal charm, didn't supply it.

When the dining-room was restored she moved to the large bedroom. White sheets had replaced the puce ones under a white brocade counterpane. Her own nightdress was under the pillow now, she slept under white lambswool blankets. The cupboard was well stocked with white linen and abundant fleecy towels. She had thrown away anything else.

The outer door banged shut, the inner door clicked. She heard heels coming up the stairway.

'Who is there? Who's that?'

'Charmian? What the heck are you doing?'

'Oh. Miss Stubbs . . . I mean . . . Violet. This is a surprise.'

'It's a surprise to me and all. Where is everything? What you been doing?'

'It is natural that you should wonder, my dear. I'll explain. Eric suggested that I should keep an eye on things here while he is away. I'm just doing what I was asked. His specific instructions were . . .'

'Instructions? Where are my things?'

'As I say, my dear, I'm doing what I was asked. I mean, dear . . . well . . . you did leave Eric, didn't you? You told him you weren't coming back. He's away at the present time, perhaps you didn't realize. Did you know that he'd gone away?'

''Course I did. To America. Teaching. I hope his conscience is bad.'

'Teaching? Did he tell you he was teaching? In the States?'

'He's a teacher, so I s'ppose he's teaching. You toe-rag, where are my things?'

'Don't call me that, dear, it's unbecoming. *You* left Eric in no uncertain terms, remember.'

Charmian was not discomforted, she was firmly in control. This moment was rather glorious, she could afford to pity the waif, looking worse now, if possible, than she had at her wedding, in a dress that clung like string. She wore fearful pointed boots. Her hair made her look like a rat.

'We had our arguments. You'd have left if you'd got what I got. And we ain't all sodding perfect like you.'

'Rudeness will accomplish nothing.'

'Fuck off. Where are my things?'

Charmian watched the girl run downstairs again. Why must she wear razor blades and such savagely black-painted brows? She followed her. Please. Understand. She'd only done what she was asked. She couldn't refuse her son. He had asked her to do some sorting. Too cluttered. Just a sort-out. Please. She'd used her own judgement. She was, after all, in the antique business, did Violet realize that?

'Not likely to forget, am I? All that tatty stuff you gave us. I had to get rid of it. Eric told me to do what I wanted. It's *our* house. Look what you done.'

'My dear . . .'

'I made it nice. Modern. It was like a museum before. Like you.'

'Please, Violet . . .'

'Please what?'

'I understood that you had left permanently.'

'Well here I am back. See?'

Charmian smoothed her blouse cuff. There was absolutely no need to justify her actions to the preposterous waif. She was cornered, shouting, swearing. The waif was routed because her temper was lost. The gods make angry those they wish to destroy. Poor mopsy, she could almost pity her, she had no retaliatory weapon. It was back to Shadwell for her. It might be a kindness to give her some of Eric's books. Perhaps she should have kept the plastic piano for her to have in Shadwell. She was getting a Steinway for Eric.

'Just wait until Ivy hears.'

'Ivy? Ah yes, your mother.'

'She's my Mum, yes. And she cares for me.'

'You obviously depend on her.'

'What d'you mean? Depend? Ivy's lovely.'

'You depend on her approval. How old are you, my dear?'

She remembered the woman as an uncontrolled weeping person, wearing too tight shoes. She had no desire ever to confront her again.

'You can talk. You kept Eric tied, didn't you? Always ringing each other. He's always talking about you. He's a Mummy's boy all right. Sick.'

'Be quiet, Violet. How dare you.'

'I'll dare what I fancy. It's true.'

'Listen to me, my dear. You know nothing about mother-hood, you don't understand how it feels. Eric is sensitive. We have always been close.'

'I know what Eric is. I married him. And I know how Ivy feels about me. She loves me in a normal way. 'Course she isn't guilty, *she* never done me no harm.'

'Harm? What do you mean? Pray explain what you mean, please.'

'I'd be praying if I was you. For forgiveness. My Ivy never took no pills before *I* was born. *I* haven't got half a hand.'

Charmian hit her before she could stop herself. She heard the impact, felt her palm sting, saw the shock on the face of the waif. Charmian hated her at that moment, more than she'd ever hated anyone. The waif had made her lose control. And she was laughing at her.

'That proves it. You never did like me, I knew it. I never thought you'd hit me, though. That's where Eric gets his violence.'

'Please . . . I didn't intend . . . my dear . . . you don't understand. My son has a great talent.'

'Talent? I'll say he has. A talent for getting violent. Shall I say what he done to me? Shall I?'

'Not just now, dear. As you may guess, I regret your marriage to my son.'

'I regret marrying him. And him supposed to be a teacher. He's an animal.'

'He has another career in view. Other avenues.'

'He can go where he sodding wants.'

'I am speaking of literature. Eric's project in the States.'

'Oh, books. You lot are no better than us. You just think you are. I saw your face when you bashed me. You might be posh and educated, inside you're the same as us. Well I hate books, see? I like doing things, not reading. I can't help it if I don't like to read.'

'Books are necessary to life, my dear. Eric is going to go far.'

While the waif tried to justify the Stygian depths of her ignorance Charmian had had time to collect herself. She deplored her own lapse. She had received unusual provocation; that didn't excuse her. The sooner the waif left the premises the better. She must get on with the work.

She anticipated the time when the waif's face would be blanked from her memory.

'Go far? He should go to the nick. He's a cruel man.'

'He is incapable of cruelty in either thought or deed.'

'Sod that. He hurt me and he hurt Dick.'

'Dick?'

'My cat. I took him with me, back home. Only Dad is allergic to him.'

Charmian concealed a smile of triumph. The poor waif, bolting back to Shadwell with her hair in purple tufts, her cat clutched in her arms, only to find Mr Stubbs didn't want her. The waif was made less than welcome because of the fur of a cat. No wonder she'd been bad tempered. Her purple gate had gone. She was disorientated.

'My dear, I just wanted to help.'

'Help? Where is everything? You've been touching and taking my things. You been in my cupboards too? My things.'

'Just . . . replacements. Just doing what Eric asked.'

'If you ask me you're a – '

'Was that a knock at the door?'

'Most probably it's Ivy. Just wait until she hears.'

Charmian waited while the waif went to the door. She had no wish to meet Mrs Stubbs, particularly at this moment. She sensed that the waif felt uncomfortable. Could it be that the waif was ashamed of her mother underneath her emotional need? The woman was shouting through the letterbox, with regrettable vowel sounds, while the waif fiddled with the lock.

'Wait, Ivy. Hold on. I can't turn it. It's stuck.'

'Come on, Vee. Don't fiddle about. I'm froze.'

She heard them whispering then. Ivy asked in a louder tone what had happened to the name on the gate. What had gone wrong with everything, the house looked different. Wishing again that she was Lady Caive-Propp, Charmian came down the stairs with a breezy gesture of her hand.

'What a pleasant surprise, Mrs Stubbs. Before you start questioning, I can explain everything. There has been a slight misunderstanding. You see my son asked me . . .'

'Your son? Yes, what about your son? He's treated my Vee

64

very bad.'

'Plus she hit me round the face, Ivy. Look. Here. Eric gets his violence from her.'

'What? You been hitting her as well, Mrs Propp? That's all I need to know. She's not been brought up to be hit. Never once did Ches nor I lay a hand.'

'The name is Caive-Propp, Mrs Stubbs. I lost my temper momentarily. It was remiss of me. I repent. In defence I have to say that Violet was unpardonably rude. I would prefer to forget the whole episode.'

'Forget? I dare say you would. Mind you, my Vee can be rude. I accept that. But hitting. Is there a history of violence in your family? If so, we ought to know.'

'A history of . . . what? *My* family. Really, Ivy – I may call you Ivy? What ever can you mean?'

'I mean what I say. If there is we ought to know. Especially just now.'

'"Just now"? Pray what do you mean exactly?'

'Just now, at the present time. Because of Vee being on for a kid. Surely you knew. Mean to say Eric didn't tell you? Mean to say you don't know?'

'No. No. I didn't know.'

'Well you know now. Mind you, it's a job to know if to be pleased or not, the way it's all turning out. I got a turn coming here to this place. Everything all changed and strange.'

'My things . . . my nice purple things.'

'Please . . . Ivy . . . Violet . . . both of you. Am I to understand that you, Violet, are pregnant? Pregnant with my son's child? Is this true?'

'What d'you mean "My son's child"? You saying my Vee is free? She's a good Catholic girl, she had a Catholic wedding. I kept her fresh, I did.'

'Yes, yes. I quite understand. But is she pregnant now? Without any question?'

'Yes I am. Sod it. Least I was when I was at the clinic,

65

suppose I still am. I don't want his kid, nor anyone else's.'

'Vee, don't speak like that. What a way to talk. It's what you got married for.'

Charmian felt ill again. Was the spell no use after all? Here was the waif insinuating herself back into the house. Was the Caive-Propp line under threat still? She told the mother and daughter quietly that Eric had said nothing to her. She had seen him off at the airport when he'd had other things on his mind. How long had Violet known this? She felt a pain in her chest as she spoke. 'Take it easy,' her practitioner had warned. Was this just a trick conceived by Ivy and the waif to get sympathy? A Caive-Propp child with Stubbs blood in it? Unthinkable. Poisonous. No.

'Hey, Vee, your mother-in-law looks poorly. Sit down, put your head down. There. Probably hearing about Vee's bun. Gave her a turn, I dare say.'

'Bun? I beg your pardon?'

'Vee's baby. Gave you a turn.'

'I do apologize, silly of me. I've been overdoing things. My doctor . . . heavy work.'

'Heavy work? I never asked you to touch my things here. My piano . . . Where's my gun?'

'Vee, don't shout like that, she's poorly. Get her some water, do.'

'She's not poorly when it comes to interfering. The toe-rag, she's stealing my house.'

'Don't be so rude. Let her explain. Here, Charmian, drink this.'

'I was asked . . . tidy, dispose . . . saw fit. My son . . . power of attorney. As you know I am an antiquarian, I own a small gallery.'

'Gallery? It's just a shop. You buy and sell like my Dad, you're not better than us, you're worse. You bash people about. I bet you stole some of my things for your sodding shop.'

'Stop it, Vee. She took a liberty, she interfered, we don't know she's a thief. Funny Eric never said nothing about the baby to her.'

'Both of you . . . please, listen. I cannot bear these scenes.'

'I'm with you there, Charmian, I hate them. Ches and I never fight.'

' "Can't bear these scenes" indeed. You started one quick enough. Bashing me and shouting. You thief, you should be in the nick. Don't you go taking her part, Ivy.'

'Vee, stop talking so rude.'

'My son . . . Eric is returning in April.'

Charmian felt really unwell. The two women were too much for her. The waif, encouraged by her mother's presence, was becoming vociferous, was shouting with savage eyes.

'You never did like me, Charmian. I'm not good enough for your son.'

'Now, Violet, please, my dear.'

'I'm not your dear, I never will be. You smile outside, inside you don't smile. Well, you needn't worry. I'm leaving Eric.'

'Don't be precipitate. A break-up would be wildly sad.'

'Liar. It's what you been hoping for.'

Charmian tried to breathe slowly, her chest hurt her, she couldn't hear well because of the noise in her ears.

'Excuse me. This giddiness . . . my practitioner . . .'

'I'll phone for a mini. Hey, Vee, what's their number?'

'Let her phone it herself. She's made herself at home here.'

'Look, Vee, it's all very well, I can understand you getting the hump, but you did walk out on Eric. Landing back home at Shadwell, upsetting Ches with that cat.'

'That's right, Ivy, now you start on me again.'

'We'll have to come to some arrangement. You can't come back home for good.'

'Why not throw me out now, Ivy? It's what you're trying to say. You don't want me no more, do you?'

'It isn't you, it's that Dick. We want you, Vee, and we want your kid. I prayed for a kiddy, I did. I bet you're thrilled underneath, eh Charmian, about the kid, I mean?'

'I . . . er . . . was surprised. I'm overjoyed, naturally, yes, of course, overjoyed.' Charmian stared and swallowed to lend credence to her words.

"Course Vee and Eric row. All couples row at first. Nothing to worry about, they row for the sake of it. It's not as if Eric had anyone else, nor Vee either.'

'Someone else?'

"Course you can't always tell with men. Men can be sneaky sometimes. Eric might have a bit on the side. What do you think, Charmian?'

Charmian put down her glass of water. She sat forward in the chair. It hadn't occurred to her that Eric, disappointed, disillusioned in the wife of his choice, might choose to look elsewhere. A brilliant solution. Naturally the waif would take it personally.

'What do you mean "someone else", Ivy? *I'm* his wife. We might row a bit, but we're faithful. Don't make me laugh.'

'Just a hunch, Vee. I'm most probably wrong. He's my son-in-law, I don't want to lose him. Marriage is made to last.'

'Well, Charmian, before you go getting any more bright ideas I may as well tell you that I possibly might move back here. This isn't your house, it's mine. And Eric's. So you can just put back all you took. My piano, my guns and all my purple towels.'

'Vee, you don't know that she pinched them. She was just doing what she was asked.'

Charmian leaned back again. The struggle to remain in ascendancy was so taxing. A child for Violet – out of the question. Another woman for Eric – a solution. But all her work here, she'd made the house so gracious again. Who would be moving in next?

'I can but repeat that Eric asked . . .'

'Well don't. We heard enough.'

'Vee, you're rude and you're cheeky. Charmian's feeling bad. Excuse her, Charmian, she's spoiled as I said. You shouldn't ought to have touched things here. I hardly recognize it now. Good job Vee can stand up for herself.'

'I rather doubt that she can. At the first hint of altercation she goes running back to you.

'Altar what? She's a good Catholic girl. I was in favour of that wedding, we all knew you weren't. Plus we all noticed your bad manners.'

'Bad manners? My bad manners, Charmian?'

'You at Vee's wedding, creeping off out of the church. Too stuck up to stay there. Ches and I thought it most rude. We were upset about it.'

Charmian had lost. She couldn't control either the mother or the daughter. She had hit the waif, pregnant with Eric's child. Her bad manners in the church had been noticed by Ivy and her low-born family. She hoped that Eric had found someone else.

CHAPTER EIGHT

Eric

The seat tipped backwards when you pressed a lever. Apart from his legs being a little cramped, Eric had no complaints. The airline people had to pack in as many passengers as possible. He had kept his mind on Charmian as they'd risen in the air. He could picture her face, smiling and unlined under her dark fur toque. She had waved her small gloved hand in farewell. She had angelic hands, she wore beautiful hand-stitched gloves like the queen, whom she resembled in many ways: her smile, her waving, her fond concern made her a being apart. When Charmian was with him he didn't feel self-conscious about his hand.

He wasn't particularly nervous about this long flight. With Charmian to see him off his apprehension had been allayed. His domestic affairs were burdensome but the disappointment he felt for his wife increased his appreciation of Charmian. He wouldn't and couldn't worry about Violet at this moment, nor could he speculate about her pregnancy. Long-term problems must be shelved until he was back in England. He'd said nothing to Charmian about the affair, no point in upsetting her too. He'd given her the house keys, she was going straight there from the airport. She wanted to tidy for him, keep it warm for his return. Now, high over the Atlantic, Violet seemed unimportant. And anything could happen, she could lose the child, if indeed she were having one. Mistakes did occur. True she had looked most unwell when he'd seen her in

Shadwell before he came away. He'd gone there to inform her that any decisions regarding their future should be left until his return. She had looked especially beautiful as she leaned against her parents' cooker. She'd looked thin and pale. Her eyes, when she could manage to look away from the television on the kitchen table, had looked at him angrily. It had been Ivy who'd done the talking, informing him again about the doctor's instructions, that Violet must have rest and quiet. No one had been interested in his American trip or his reason for going there. No one had asked how he felt. He would have appreciated a little cordiality from Chester but the man had barely spoken. He'd not looked well either, had kept sneezing and scratching his wrists. He'd been glad to come away. Whether Violet was pregnant or not, she had left him, for no good reason. Let her stay away. He had Charmian, she always understood him, his interests were close to her heart. She had stood there waving as she used to wave when he'd travelled off to school, the prettiest mother with the prettiest smile, on Waterloo station. She'd be so proud one day when she sat in the stalls, watching a play by him. But first things first, he must finish 'Family Loves'. His will to succeed came from Charmian, he would dedicate it to her. He'd been a loner at school because of missing her. Charmian discouraged self-pity but he'd never forgotten his hand. It hadn't been until he joined the drama group at college that the course of his life had changed. He was practical about his ambition; student acclaim was no proving ground. He didn't want to teach all his life. The long school holidays suited him, gave him time for writing his play, but Violet spoiled everything. And yet . . . he couldn't forget the look on her face when she'd sung. 'And did the Countenance Divine shine forth upon our clouded hills? And was Jerusalem builded here among those dark Satanic mills?' Remembering her, high in the sky, he ached for her again.

He realized now that he'd gone wrong from the start, letting her make those changes. And he'd never liked her food. Buns, egg and chips soon palled. Her cat was the final straw. Naturally he longed for Charmian again, for her meals and aesthetic taste. It had taken courage to leave England with his life at this turning point.

'Excuse me, sir, can I help?'

'Help? I beg your pardon?'

He was looking up into the black eyes of a black air hostess, uniformed in green.

'Your seat belt, sir, you may unfasten it. Would you like me to assist you?'

'Oh . . . no thanks. I was almost asleep.'

'I'll be bringing the drinks by and by. Would you care for anything right now? A little orange juice? Let me unclip your belt.'

'I can manage, thanks.'

He pushed his right hand under his coat. Had she offered from pity? Had everybody seen? He'd rather stay belted up than be seen to fumble. Why had she offered him juice? She had coaxed as if he were a minor. Was it normal practice to fuss? They had been in the air for some time, he'd need to get up soon, use the toilet. He smoothed his hair with his left hand, it felt different, longer, he'd grown it for this trip. Had she been mocking him? What an exaggerated accent she had. The other passengers seemed to be indifferent to anything but the ordering of drinks and duty-free goods, scent mostly. He had smelled enough scent to last a lifetime. Too much scent was a sign of too little taste. Charmian never used it, nor, he felt sure, did the queen. He ordered a whisky, though he'd had no breakfast, he had been too tense for food. Charmian had understood, pouring him weak china tea. The hostess was smiling again. Doubtless she was trying to be kind but her painted smile didn't appeal. He was tired of paint and silly hair styles, just as he was tired of scent. He wondered if Charmian was at the house on the green now, and if she were thinking of him. He couldn't see out of the window, his seat was too far inside. He felt light in the head from the whisky. He would try and sleep a little, in this craft like a flying barn. What would that hostess be like to feel, stroke, caress? Her oiled black eyes were tender; was she black everywhere? What would she be like to . . .

'Roast lamb or goulash, sir?' her kiss-painted mouth was asking him, making him jump again. He was not in the habit of speculating about strange women, he felt disloyal to both Charmian and to his wife.

'Er . . . roast lamb, please.'

The plastic food tray, when it came, reminded him of Violet. Plastic utensils, plastic-tasting meat, a mauve plastic-looking desert. Drinking so early made him clumsy, he dropped his plastic spoon. Was Violet really having a child? Would he hold it in his arms?

'Excuse me, sir, would you like to watch the movie?'

'Movie? Is there one?'

You could hire earphones to plug into your arm rest, after they'd let down a screen for a musical of the type he most deplored, the kind *she* and her mother would have liked. The heroine had enormous eyes. There were dancing girls decked in beads, there were oriental feasts with music. Eyes flashed, thighs undulated, he watched their beautiful breasts. The heroine was small and thin with a pale skinned fragile neck. He wanted Violet; why wasn't she with him? He didn't want her, she'd get in his way. He must put women from his mind, he mustn't think of them, his wife or anyone else. He hadn't done much to please Violet, she'd not put herself out for him. He didn't pretend to genius. 'Family Loves' might not succeed. If it didn't it would not be his fault. No wives, no dancing girls, not even a mother must cloud his aims and labours. Inside he felt afraid. He could be deluding himself. Where was Violet, his wife and his love?

The enormous-eyed heroine sang, the beaded damsels

73

danced, Eric slept. He dreamed of Violet, floating up to the stars, he tried to catch her clothing, his hand encountered a claw.

He woke up to find the hostess was handing out more plastic trays, a Devon cream tea this time. 'Enjoy it,' she smiled at each passenger. Her mouth was the colour of jam. The scones tasted of soda, the jam was thick and sweet. Violet would have enjoyed it; strong tea, sweet cream and jam.

It had been dark for some hours when he climbed down from the plane that had taken him to the domestic airport near to the Writing Centre. The small plane impressed him more than the barn-like one. He'd been able to see out of it. The seven other passengers and he had watched the night scenery below. He could pick out the New England traffic, dotted necklaces of light. The distance had been short, their altitude low. He'd seen woodlands interspersed with arable land, small farms with lighted barns. Towns made patches of stronger light, cobweb bright in the dark. Rivers and small lakes glittered. America lay below him, waiting to help with his play.

He bumped his head as he got out. The other travellers walked to their waiting cars, commuters going home. He was the last. He stood on the tarmac waiting, his travel bag over his shoulder, his suitcase by his side. A wind was blowing, with rain in it, flattening and wetting his hair, drops ran down his nose. Two men with gum in their jaws checked the engine, calling out through the rain. At Kennedy airport he'd queued, he'd been quizzed and questioned, scrutinized, assessed. They had enquired the purpose of his visit, his invitation to the Centre had been unfolded, examined, passed from hand to hand. At this airport they said 'Hi' and went on chewing gum. He appreciated the quiet of the small building, the sense of space, the friendliness. His shoulder bag was heavy. A gum-chewing man took his case. Would anyone from the Centre meet him? What would they think of his hand?

'Hi. You must be Eric. I'm Fran.'

'Oh. How do you do? How did you guess it was I?'

He gave a small bow. He wouldn't shake her hand until she had seen his own hand.

'I couldn't mistake an Englisher. Here, hand me over your bag.'

'No. Thanks very much, I can manage.'

Would she have offered if she hadn't noticed it? He thought that he liked her, she had a breeziness of manner that he found reassuring. An easy-going girl who didn't stare at him. The rain blew another gust of wet over them. He needn't be shy with her, she had such a cheerful smile. He followed her. When he saw that she walked with a limp his face went smooth with relief. She understood, she knew how he felt, she had a handicap too. Perhaps she had once felt about her foot as he did about his hand. She showed no discomfiture though, humming pleasantly as she walked. Her built-up shoe clumped over the floor of the reception building. Her straight, rather greasy hair was cut in a line round her shoulders. When she looked back at him she had a slight cast in her eye. A double handicap, one eye and her foot, yet she was so relaxed.

'I beg your pardon, Fran, what were you saying?'

'I said what time did you leave London, England?'

He explained that he'd been travelling since early that day, that he had watched an indifferent musical in the larger plane to help while away the time. His brain felt unreal, as if he were still in the sky; this wasn't helped by the seven-hour difference in time. He asked her if she too were a writer. He liked her large teeth when she smiled, though they weren't particularly white. Before getting into the waiting car she put on horn-rimmed glasses. She was the deputy director, she explained, while the boss man was away. She had trained as a natural history teacher, she liked working at the Centre best. Helping writers further their work was the most worthwhile job there was. Yessir, she loved her job. Eric decided then to give up 'How do you do' in favour of 'Hi'. He wanted to be more like Fran, more direct, not so suspicious. He told her that he knew very little about wildlife, especially American wildlife. Her face glowed as she explained that the Centre had fabulous woods, a lot of wildlife, he was in for a real treat. They had six writers staying at present, all longing to meet him. They met to eat in the main hall at night and at breakfast. They slept and worked in individual cabins. She asked how his own work was progressing, coming along okay? He mustn't hesitate to ask for anything he needed. The Centre existed to provide, to serve and encourage art.

'It's marvellous meeting you, Fran,' he said, getting the courage to take her hand, squeezing it. She was the most friendly person he'd ever met, and so natural. She told him that she had liked the sample of his work that he'd sent their admissions board. He told her about 'Family Loves' and his ambition to win the competition. He wanted to leave teaching, he loved literature, he disliked teaching it. He squeezed her hand again as it lay on the driver's wheel. Not only was she friendly, she had taste and spoke her mind. He liked her large glasses and her rather smoky smell. Menthol cigarettes probably, which she kept puffing. The dinginess of her teeth must be from nicotine. The cast in her right eye didn't show under the glasses. It appeared that he was the only playwright, the other writers wrote novels or poems.

'Are you a family man, Eric?'

'I er . . . I teach, as I said. At a large London school.'

'Pardon me. Have you a wife and kids?'

'Er . . . yes. A wife.'

Did he imagine it or did she look crestfallen? Her curiosity was flattering, his brain had come down from the sky. The black air hostess wasn't on the same planet as this lovely Yankee girl. He hoped that he would meet more like her. The brown of her jersey matched the brown of her lank hair. Her shoes were the kind worn by climbers, just the thing for a built-up heel.

'Well, Eric, I believe in you, that's for sure. We're real happy to have someone from London, England to come visit us.'

He stretched his legs out, turning to her, enjoying his ride through the dark. No need to instruct or talk down to this girl. *She* didn't plaster her hair into tails or wear razor blades round her neck. She'd never mock him or sneer. He felt that she'd understand his admiration for Charmian. He'd heard that Americans loved their mothers as much as they loved their flag. They were uncomplicated, loyal, as wholesome as apple pie. She was a gift from the stars.

CHAPTER NINE

Eric

They were driving along one of the roads that he'd looked down on from the sky, when he'd craned his head to see America. Now he and Fran were one of the twinkling dots in the necklaces of light. Fran drove the car fast and well. No traffic jams or bad surfaces here, she explained; tolls were extracted at interstate points to help maintain the roads. They drove through the dark without speaking again. He felt companionable, as if they'd been friends for years. They turned into a wide driveway. 'Penn Center' the sign said. This long tree-lined avenue with the white painted building at the end of it would be his home for a month. It was less imposing than the brochure had implied, not as large but tidy and trim. There were the white steps to the veranda, a porch lamp swung in the rain.

Fran banged the car door. No, she said, she'd take his luggage now, it was her duty and pleasure. He was the writer, remember? The staff existed to serve. For the duration of his stay he must devote all his energy to the pursuit of his craft. He liked hearing his play referred to as his craft. Such deference gave him confidence. She obviously had no inkling of his own inner doubts. He followed her up the steps.

'Hi, folks. Here is our Englisher, all the way from London, England, at last.'

His colleagues for the coming month were grouped round a log fire. Two of them lounged on a settle, the rest sat on the floor. He was looking at the faces of the literary cream of the States, all wearing horn-rims like Fran. Their clever eyes welcomed him.

'Hi.'

He cleared his throat.

'Oh. Hi. How do you do? I'm Eric Caive-Propp. I've come here to write a play.'

He would soon pick up their expressions and understand their ways. This was how he'd felt the first time he'd stood before an English class, inadequate, afraid. But these men were writers like him, on his side, wishing him well. He didn't have to teach them, or impart knowledge or good taste, very likely he'd learn from them. What a good thing he'd grown his hair. They were all dressed casually, like Fran. He had packed his cords and a sports jacket, he had a pullover like Fran's. He wanted their acceptance, to look and sound like them.

The low room looked like a ranch house with a rag mat on the floor. There were trestle tables, logs in a basket, a lovely woodsmoke smell. No one stood up. Should he join them on the floor, a habit he'd never acquired? He didn't want to be thought stuck-up. He held his deformed hand behind him. He felt Fran's hand, touching him, stroking his wrist with light strokes. He smiled then at the writers' faces, emboldened to talk of his play. The man in the check shirt puffed a billow of smoke at him. What was his play to be called? Eric explained about 'Family Loves', his half-hour radio play.

'Neat idea. Broad spectrum.'

'I need to submit it when I get back to England. I've come here to get some peace, away from ties and interruptions.'

'Eric has a wife back in London, England,' Fran explained to them.

He blushed, unused to talking about his work or his secret hopes, except to Charmian. He wanted to hear about their work and their loved ones, their president and their love of home-baked pies. The man in the check shirt puffed again.

After having had three wives he could sympathize with Eric, he was a poet himself. The man on his left was a novelist who had just had a break-up with his girl. Eric felt his knees tremble. He belonged here, with the literati of the west.

'I . . . I . . .' He started choking.

Fran interrupted, her left eye looking at the company, her right eye looking at him. 'Look, fellas, this poor guy is bushed. He's been in the air all day. He hasn't eaten, he's coming with me now. This way, Eric, it's orders. You're coming with me. Yessir.'

She took his wrist, leading him to the kitchen at the other end of the hall. He would see the other guys in the morning, right now he must eat and rest. There was dumpling and vegetable hotpot, there was green salad on the side. Did he like cheese with his oatcakes? There was herbal tea if he liked. They didn't believe in coffee here, except the decaffeinated kind; wholefoods home cooked was the aim at Penn Center. To that end they grew vegetables. They used to keep hens for their eggs, but had given up because of the wild animals that prowled round the coops. In Fran's view you were what you ate. Did he like yoghurt? Simple meals, carefully prepared; no alcohol nourished the spirit too. Eric nodded eagerly. She mustn't know of his quite recent longings for pheasant, jugged hare in wine sauce, caviar. He'd recently turned tee-total he said, helping himself lavishly to green salad, a food which both he and Violet never ate; about the only taste they shared. All that would change now, thanks to Fran. He bit into a celery stalk, trying to eat quietly. She poured his decaffeinated coffee into a pottery mug. This place was homely in the right kind of way. Ethnically satisfying, in touch with nature, this was the way to live. Violet's attempts at cooking, trashy buns, soda pop were the other side of the world. Scrubbed pine, check curtains, an old-fashioned range with friendly Fran behind it were all that a writer could need. He could think of Violet without an ache now, nor did he miss Charmian. He was breaking his English ties. It was peculiar that Fran smoked so much, but everyone had flaws, it showed she was human.

She told him that the woods were very dark, this rain would make them darker. She hoped he'd remembered his flashlight.

'Tonight? I didn't realize we slept in the cabins. Nobody mentioned a torch.'

It seemed she had forgotten to send the list of items he would need during his stay here. A sleeping bag for his cabin, a radio, top boots for the wet as well as a strong flashlight. Insect repellent was needed when the weather became warmer. The woods were unforested, you could easily get lost. She asked if he liked walking.

'I never did much of it. No sports of any kind. My . . . handicap, you know. Mind you, Fran, with the right companion . . .'

She offered him her own sleeping bag. The staff slept in the main building, she didn't need it. His cabin was remote from the rest, the most solitary. He would soon get used to the woods. They ate home-baked cookies from a tin, smiling at each other. He told her of his inexperience of life in the country. He loved what he'd seen so far.

'I guess we should go to your cabin now, Eric. You need a good night's rest.'

In the main hall his colleagues were still talking. He caught the words 'abstract expressionism', 'concrete art', 'Fauvism' through thick clouds of smoke. He'd have liked to have stayed to listen. He couldn't remember their names though he'd been introduced. The man with the check shirt and the Meerschaum pipe was the most friendly. He called out after Eric. Did they keep Mothering Sunday in London, England? They took the day seriously here.

Outside Fran took his arm, steering him down the wet driveway. He held her torch in his left hand, she carried the sleeping bag. It was a good half-an-hour's walk, she said. It was raining steadily, the sound of the rain was broken by drips from the trees. They turned down a muddy track overhung with growth. Wet twigs pulled at their clothes. Fran's fingers found his sleeve, her cold hair touched his cheek. She was better than the light of her torch. There was no moon, no stars, you couldn't see where the trees ended and the sky began. The path got narrower still, twisting sharply. They came to a marshy patch with duckboards to walk on. They slipped and clung closer, negotiating the mud. They had to bend even lower to enter a runway, as small as an animal trail, through dense bushes. Branches pricked his face. He tripped on a root, hurting his knee. At last they could stand upright again. He shone the torch round a small clearing, the cabin was in the middle. It had a stout door, a slate roof and a chimney.

Fran took a huge key from her pocket. There was an inside door made of wire mesh against the insects in the summer months. She felt inside for the light switch. An unshaded bulb hung from a flex in the centre of the hut.

'This is your cabin, Eric. This is where you sleep and work.'

'It's . . . very fine, Fran. Very fine indeed.'

His dwelling was a single room with a table and chair in it. No curtains, a wooden floor scoured almost white exaggerated the sound of their feet. He hadn't dreamed of anything so rudimentary. Was this called 'living rough'?

'It's . . . er . . . where do I sleep?'

Behind the door was a pallet raised from the floor on a board. She put down the sleeping bag. 'Bucolic', that was the word for it, this was how the early settlers lived. He repeated how fine it was. She lit the newspaper in the stone hearth, she threw on some sticks and then logs. Slowly the flames took over, the paper smelled of damp. Smoke blew over them in billows, ash fell, feathery soft. He remembered how they'd thrown rice at Violet and himself after the wedding, how it settled in her purple lace. He didn't miss her now. The flames started making the sticks snap. A shower of twigs fell down the chimney, and then a shower of leaves.

'It's only birds. This cabin hasn't been in use for a while. I thought being British and reserved you'd appreciate it. The birds nest in the chimney. I'm quite a bird freak myself.'

'I like them too, Fran. I like most animals. I'm not so keen on pets. That is domestic ones.'

Fran said that people should respect nature, consideration should be granted to all living things. He marvelled at how much they had in common, both of them liking nature, both liking wholesome food. Their attitudes, the way they faced life in spite of handicaps, were similar. They both had sensitive minds. Meeting her was a delight, he was so glad that she didn't paint.

'Paint? How come, Eric? I don't understand you.'

'I mean . . . you don't paint your face. I do so dislike it.'

'Gee, Eric. I'm liberated. I have no time for outward show.'

'You're so right. You couldn't be improved.'

Her dingy teeth, her smokiness, and – now that they were warm in the cabin – her unmistakeable smell of sweat were distinctive. She was beautiful in her own way. Earthy, that was the word. He told her that he also disliked people who thought themselves better than others, who held the rest in contempt.

'You mean snobs, don't you? I thought that Englishers were big on snobs. We Yanks can be brash. Some of us think big is beautiful.'

The fire burned well. They warmed themselves. He held out his right hand timidly, not wanting the firelight shining on it. She had rather bitten nails he saw. She pointed to where he could wash, behind a cubicle in the corner where there was a single tap. His lavatory was outside, an earth closet down a track. He said nothing. He'd get used to it. There was a hotplate for heating a saucepan. The Centre provided lunches, hot soups and stews for the writers to take away. The Centre was there to serve, to help and encourage art, she repeated. Her cross-eyes looked warm with kindness. Here then was the sleeping bag. She would leave him now to his dreams.

'Fran. How can I thank you?'

'It's my pleasure. Don't try, finish your play. That's reward enough for me, Eric. I'll find my way back to the house.'

She wouldn't let him walk back with her, she was used to the twisting paths. She could manage the low branches and muddy duckboards. Goodnight. Pleasant dreams.

He was alone now, really alone. He'd felt alone at 'Purple Rest', though Violet was there; this aloneness was another kind. In a wood, in the heart of a far country, in damp cold and dripping rain. Rain drummed on the roof over his head, he heard it hiss on the embers in the hearth. The fire burned fast, you had to keep feeding it, the feathery ash was gone. He rubbed his eyes. The reflection in the uncurtained window showed a man with an odd-shaped hand trying not to feel solitary, rubbing his stinging eyes. Had Fran got back safely to the main building? He peered through the pane again. Behind his cubicle his tap dripped, slower than the dripping outside. He heard a scurrying noise. Wolves or bears? Danger? He was too tired to care. In England privacy mattered, he hated being anywhere without the curtains closely drawn. He'd have to change here. He felt as if the wet branches were watching him, night creatures, even lunatics. He'd ignore such thoughts, he'd remember sensible Fran clumping her way through the night now, regardless of twigs plucking her hair.

And she'd left something of herself, something intimate. He sniffed the sleeping bag. He could smell her particular smell, menthol smoke mixed with sweat, and on looking closely he saw a long fine greasy hair. He would place his head where hers had been, before drawing the zip to his chin. He wondered if she slept naked. Pyjamas were more likely, he thought, fleecy ones, navy or brown. And her foot, was it . . . curious? What was she like without clothes?

Behind the cubicle there were a few square feet of privacy, out of reach of the night outside. There was a hook for his clothes to hang on, a shelf with a tooth glass, two toilet rolls, a piece of wrapped soap. He had no complaints about the cleanliness here, but the draining system was primitive. In the morning he would have to empty his enamel washing bowl into the drain outside. He warmed some water in a saucepan and washed with the piece of plain soap. He had light, heat, water, space to work in, he had food provided by Fran. He couldn't ask for anything more. Perhaps he'd been over-indulged before. Nothing worthwhile was achieved without sacrifice. Perhaps he'd not suffered enough. He combed back his longish hair, did his pyjamas up. He didn't expect to sleep well. He lay breathing the faint smell of sweatiness, the stronger smell of smoke.

He woke up before it was light. He was in a hut in a wood in America, surrounded by trees and birds. Small tapping sounds moved overhead, not rain now. There was that scurrying sound. Probably the birds were hopping on the roof, pecking for seeds. As it grew light he could make out the tree branches, birches and pines mostly. Fran had told him there were chipmunks and woodchucks here. Squirrels were common-place. He wasn't nervous now it was light again, the sun was beginning to shine. The sleeping bag was cosy, the hut was inspiring. He could do without cushions, hot pipes and rugs. Frugality had charm. He ran down the track in his pyjamas to the earth closet – well, he'd get used to that.

The fireplace was cold now, he heard the rustles up the chimney, those birds were early at work. He shaved, soaping his long pale cheeks. Now he thought about it, the rest were all wearing beards. He might grow one as well. He was glad that they were all men, fewer distractions for him. He'd modify his accent as well, using their expressions, he wanted to be liked by them. He washed with his ivory soap again, he cleaned and relaid his fire. He had much to learn; he'd never been a boy scout. He pushed the poker up the chimney to make more dirt and leaves fall. He thought he heard cheeping, he mustn't hurt them. He felt full of goodwill and beneficence. His beard would soon grow here.

He shut his door, locking it. What was Violet doing now? Did she miss him? Was she wondering? Was she going to have a child?

The robins in his clearing were the size of hens, almost, blood-red breasted and button-eyed. This was America, where big was beautiful and bird-song extra loud. A toad the size of a rat watched him, he heard a woodpecker tap. The sun was already quite warm on his shoulders as he bent into the animal trail. The branches were steaming a little, a heavy-tailed animal loped in front. Was it a woodchuck? A branch snapped back into his face, his shoes got soaked again. At the other end of the trail he stood upright, now for the duckboards and mud. Another toad hopped across his path, two squirrels ran over his head along branches dotted with raindrops, more smaller necklaces of light. He'd need to buy boots.

'Hi, Eric.'

'Er . . . hi. Hello. Hi.'

CHAPTER TEN

Eric

His colleagues, the literary cream of the States, talked about their output, their daily pain of producing a lot of words. Agony was a popular topic, as well as how many words. They discussed typewriters, ribbons, dictionaries, their availability and cost. Their eyes looked rapt when they talked of their labours, they kept asking Fran when she was going to town for fresh supplies of foolscap. Because of the remote location she didn't go frequently. Eric listened uncomfortably to all this. Under no circumstances must they find out how he spent his time. How, day after day, he sat at his table staring out at the trees. He kept meaning to start pecking industriously with five fingers on the portable machine lent him by Fran; he could go fast if he concentrated. The lid stayed on the typewriter, he wrote nothing but a few commas, inserting them into his opening speech, removing them at night. 'Family Loves' hadn't grown at all. He was too fascinated by the woods outside to continue it, he didn't want to miss the chance of seeing brown bears or porcupines as well as more outsized birds. He delighted in the scurries of the squirrels. Sometimes, as a change from watching nature, he sat and stared at his hand. It looked so peculiar holding a pen, writing a comma with it, taking it away. This was what they meant by birth pains, this difficulty day after day. He wouldn't call it agony exactly but he preferred watching wildlife. How could his play be accepted if nothing got put on the page? He hadn't even got the words in his head, he really had no right to be here. Compared to literary cream he was just skimmed milk. What ever would Fran say?

Her meals were excellent and mouth-watering, he didn't deserve them, nor did he deserve the lunch baskets that were given out to take back to the cabins each day. He felt fraudulent as he hurried down the leafy tracks, bent under the tunnel, the basket in his left hand. Back in the cabin his first task was to look at his lunch. Rich soups in wide-necked flasks, whole-grain sandwiches, yoghurt, fruit. He liked to think that Fran took special pains with his baskets. She knew he liked interesting cheeses. Her sleeping bag continued to be a joy.

On the first morning he had found a packet under his basket lid, with a note. 'Here is a clean cover for the sleeping bag. Hope you enjoy your lunch.' Such concern was endearing. He couldn't bring himself to take her used cover off, it was a part of her. He put the clean one under the dirty one to keep the scent of hair and smoke. At night in bed he wasn't quite alone; he breathed the fragrance of Fran.

He enjoyed keeping the cabin tidy; he'd never done house-work before. Life with Violet had little order; she disliked work and routine. Each morning now, after he'd checked the contents of his lunch basket, he swept out his cabin with a broom. He dusted the table, smoothed Fran's sleeping bag before scrubbing the grey stone hearth. With his lunch spread out by the typewriter the world felt very fine. He was king of his little castle, his kingdom was the wood. For the time being the animals of the wood were his main concern, he studied them constantly. Their activities put him to shame. They organized their lives so well, keeping busy, only pausing for sleep or food. He kept a look out for woodchuck, he'd only seen one once, with its mild face and large tail. He saw a huge hedgehog sniffing at the tree roots; Fran was right, big was beautiful, wildlife here was noisy and flash. His fire was an occasional nuisance, smoking a lot, fresh rubbish fell each night. He didn't push the poker up again, those birds had squatters' rights. Sometimes nutshells showered down.

The weather turned colder again, the wet early spring turned wintry. Then it snowed. He didn't object, his kingdom was even more beautiful when it was virgin white. He pushed his table nearer to the fire, wore two vests under his shirt. He took the lid off the typewriter, ready to make a start. He pushed down the comma, the key caught up in a hole in the ribbon. He tried to unwind the spool. He wished he had Fran here to help him. He wished she would do his typing. He wished there was something to type. She hadn't been able to make her trip to the town because of this fall of snow. He needed boots badly now. He needed a typewriter ribbon. That morning at breakfast she'd offered to lend him a book on American birds in the wild. She loved them, they were her speciality, her main reason for working here – and to help writers, of course. He told her he wanted to study them, that birds were his latest interest since coming to the resort. He kept a watch for them as he hurried to the main building each morning. Fran's smile behind the percolator brought him more luck for the coming day. The man in the check shirt continued to be the friendliest. He asked Eric if he thought that London poets suffered as dearly as he did. Eric thought they did, though in fact few living poets had come his way. He was more concerned with watching Fran behind the serving hatch than check shirt's miserable pangs. Did she give each one of them that special smile, did she touch each writer's wrist? Check shirt had the effrontery to pull her hair as he offered his cup to be filled. Eric longed to snatch the pipe from his teeth and sever him with an axe. Arrogant overdressed dog. He seized his lunch basket and left without saying goodbye. It was Fran's job to be cordial, he knew that. The truth was he didn't fit in. Life was basic, unpretentious, honest, they were kind enough to him. The truth was, he couldn't write.

The wood haunted his imagination, at night he still felt afraid. He stared out at it, long and hard. Familiarity, that was the key. He wanted to explore the far pathways, so far he hadn't the nerve. Returning to his cabin each evening in the darkness was difficult enough. The torch battery went dead. He would enjoy a stroll with Fran under those conifers while they breathed the snowy air. He'd enjoy pointing the stars out. The constellations were timeless, he knew she'd feel as he did. Violet never cared, lurking indoors with her cat. He continued to sleep deeply and well in the sleeping bag.

Before he'd arrived at the Centre he'd been satisfied with the theme of his play 'Family Loves'. The family was the pivot on which you succeeded or failed, the fulcrum where love was learned. His idea seemed so puny now. He didn't fool himself, he was no genius, he hoped to succeed by hard work. But he couldn't work. Fran had faith in him, he mustn't let her down. Perhaps his title was wrong. 'Family Loving', 'Changing Loves', 'Astonished Love'. Yes, love was astonishing. He'd not had enough of it so far. Love changed, that he did know. His love for Charmian, wonderful Charmian, was different from what he'd felt for Violet, his wife and once his love. Absurd love, unsuitable love, unnatural love. Unacceptable. Fran came as another chance. He wondered if she were passionate, as fervid and insatiable as Violet. Her forearm under her brown jersey had thick fair hair like fur. Passionate women often were hairy. He was at a crossroads, almost an impasse. He hated teaching, he was disappointed in marriage, he disliked children, even those from good homes. He didn't understand them, didn't want to, they tended to laugh at his hand. He'd no intention of writing about children, his characters would all be mature. Love attracted him, he wanted to write about it. Astonishing, upsetting, changing. Everyone searched for it. If you found it, love often slipped away. He'd ask Fran what she thought about it. Dialogue came easily to him, that was the irony. Why should he feel so stuck? He'd always understood that if you were dogged, progress would ensue. Perhaps he didn't know his characters well enough.

He'd thought until now that he did, those five people and their dog were part of him, as real as his day-to-day life.

The noise on the roof persisted, the squirrels stayed alert, regardless of snow. They ran across, jumped the branches, they raced round and round the cabin. The chipmunks had gone to ground again, caught out by the false spring. He'd not spotted that orange lizard again either, he must ask Fran about that. The birds here had imaginative names; chickadee, whip-o'er-will, mocking bird. How perfect life would be if it weren't for the play. Dreaming out of the window, cleaning his cabin, spotting wildlife while eating his lunch made the days pass so pleasantly. He crumbled food on to the stones outside his doorway, hoping that the woodchuck might appear. He gathered kindling, dragging the snow-covered sticks over the clearing, knocking them clean on his step. Frosted wood burned beautifully. He did his own washing, hanging his socks and shirts over a berry bush, like those shapes in the 'Purple Rest' yard. But Violet owned the latest washing machine. She'd never had to rub a cake of soap over clothing, before rinsing it under one tap, nor had she to wring it out in a clearing in the heart of a dense wood. 'Purple Rest' had a waste disposer. He had to bury any scraps if the squirrels disliked his fare. Fran actually wanted to help him, that's what he'd always missed. He'd had Charmian of course, but she was a mother. Violet had never cared. What was she doing at this moment? She could have miscarried by now. Would their marriage continue? Did he still want it? Did he want Fran for good?

By the third week at Penn Center he was in a panic. Had they guessed he was a fraud? He wished he could understand the literary cream a little better, they were friendly but a world apart still. They liked to read early drafts of their manuscripts by the light of their wood fire. Listening to long sections of novels or poems after supper made Eric faint with distaste. One evening he could stand the company no longer, he wouldn't stay listening until bedtime as the rest of the writers did, he'd go back to his cabin early. And this time he would work. He wouldn't get up from his table until he'd written something. He pulled up his chair and sat down. He heard footsteps outside in the dark. A prowler? A bear? Fran?

'Oh, Fran. It's you. If you knew how I've been longing . . .'

'Hi, Eric. I promised you my bird book. And here are some boots, size ten. Okay?'

He repeated how thoughtful she was, how he appreciated her. No more wet feet for him. The boots she'd bought were like hers, a sensible snuff-coloured brown. And she looked so cold, snow was clinging to her hair and shoulders, flakes caught in the knitted wool. She shook her head, she liked helping, it was her job, remember? The staff were here to serve. How was his play coming?

'That's just it, Fran. I'm ashamed.'

'How come? Ashamed?'

'I've written so little. I've written nothing at all. I've been wasting time. Please, let me make you some tea.'

She said a cup of tea would be neat. He was right, she had got chilled. He said he'd been longing to see her alone. Sit down, she was all wet. He put his chair near to the fireside. She must take her boots off. She smiled. He was being real sweet to her. If he wasn't careful she'd be wanting to come visit him, in London, England, one day.

'I'd really love you to, Fran. Meanwhile . . . you're with me now. Er . . . I'm married, as I said. Here in the cabin, we can be alone.'

'Sure thing. You did tell me. Happily married?'

'Not too happily, I'm afraid. Violet and I . . . well, we're not as happy as we might be.'

'That's tough. You mean, you don't relate? You can't communicate? You mean she gives you a hard time? How come?'

'That's it. One way and another she gives me a very hard

time.'

'Gee. You'll divorce?'

'It isn't settled. I'm not certain yet. I came here to think things over. And to write my play, of course. I didn't imagine I'd ever meet someone like you. You see, my wife has no taste.'

'You mean she can't taste her food? Gee.'

'I mean she lacks discernment. No vision, no idea of true worth.'

'She doesn't encourage your work?'

'Oh no. Not at all. Nor my teaching.'

He was betraying Violet who knew nothing about the play. But Fran must realize his need. His house was ghoulish, a nightmare. She asked him again, how come?

'No rest. No tranquillity. Loud pop music. And everything in it smells.'

'Of anything in particular? Cooking?'

'She doesn't cook. She buys chips. It's . . . well, violets, Parma violets. Her name is Violet, you see. She's obsessed with cheap ornaments, bric-à-brac. At school functions she lets me down. People notice. She looks like a . . . I can't tell you.'

'A real shame. You deserve the best.'

'She can't love properly, that's at the root of it. She's never learned to give.'

'She loves no one? Nobody in the world?'

'No person. She loves her cat. And her mother, of course. She prefers the cat to me.'

Fran said that Violet couldn't be entirely bad if she loved animals and her Mom. She'd loved the cat at the Centre, which ran away when they got rid of the hens.

'You don't understand, Fran. She's not normal. I'm convinced of it. The cat smells to the heavens and dribbles. She keeps it in our bed.'

'I guess the poor kitty needs affection. It's unhygienic, I agree.'

'Oh it is. She's not hygienic, the house isn't very clean. She spends all her time on herself. And her hair . . . honestly, Fran.'

'Gee. Eric. Hon.'

He tried to explain about Violet, her hair, her clothes, her mind. The ugly purples she affected, her razor blades and paint.

Fran nodded understandingly, touching his wrist again. She wriggled her feet in her thick socks, holding them out to the heat. He loved the feel of her near him. He mustn't rush her; he longed to remove her clothes. He must move cautiously, mustn't alarm her. In a whisper he told her that they shared so much, their outlooks were similar, she deserved the finest life. Er . . . now for the tea. Milk and sugar? She said she liked it weak.

While she sipped he told her about his nervousness, especially at night. The noises and tappings bothered him. It wasn't so much the activity as the sensation of being watched. He didn't mind birds in the chimney. He hated being watched.

'Gee, Eric. I thought you liked solitude. The Britishers' reserve. I thought you'd like this cabin.'

'Now you're here in it, I'm quite happy. I adore the wildlife, as you know.'

He told her about the huge hedgehog he'd seen, and that red lizard in the sun. Would they survive this snow-fall? Fran's eyes warmed with concern. The way to her heart was via nature study. She could teach him a lot, she said.

'But, Fran, I'll be leaving soon.'

'Don't say that, Eric. Stay on here a while.'

He told her he must return, much as he loved it here. He had commitments, responsibilities back in England. It felt exquisite to have her hair near his again, real hair joined to her head, not loose on a sleeping bag. It was exquisite to hear her sipping tea. She said that the staff were not supposed to visit the visitors in their cabins, particularly at night. She'd only come tonight to bring his boots. The boss man would soon be back;

she'd taken a chance. The boss thought that too much fraternization discouraged the flow of work. The staff were there to serve, not hinder. Perhaps he'd prefer a cabin nearer the main hall. He shook his head. He must see more of her; no one would ever find out.

'But your play, hon. I'd never forgive myself.'

He had to explain then that she had become his play, she had taken its place in his heart. And the wildlife, of course. Since coming here all he'd done was put in a few commas. All day he sat at the window, trying to spot squirrels and birds. He ate a lot and thought of her constantly. Literature had long been his subject, he loved words, spoken or read. Now he was a pretender, his imagination was blocked. As well, he'd lost his nerve.

'You shouldn't throw in the towel so easy. You've had a troubled life. You need a rest.'

'Oh I have. A troubled life. You're absolutely right. We both have, Fran. I can tell.'

Her eyes looked desolate. He'd touched on an echoing pain. They were twin souls and she felt it. He touched her neck under the hair. He must move slowly and with the utmost care. She was trembling. Fran was terrified.

'Take off your glasses. Let me. You have the prettiest eyes, Fran. Don't cry. What have I done? It's my hand, isn't it?'

'No. No.'

'What is it? Please, you must say.'

'My eyes. My astigmatism. It's so noticeable. As if that wasn't bad enough there's my foot. I'm not pretty, I know I'm a freak.'

'You? *You*? You mean me. I thought you hated me to touch you, because of my ugly hand. You have pretty eyes. I hardly noticed your foot.'

'I limp. People stare. I'm homely. I feel like the most unwanted woman alive.'

'That's nonsense and you know it. I do know what you

mean though. You have to sublimate shortcomings.'

'How come you're so understanding?'

He told her that he knew how bitter life could be. People's sneers could be more painful than living with the object of their sneers, in his case his hand.

'The intimate side of things, Eric, that's another problem. I hardly dare to take off my clothes.'

Forcing himself to be bold he asked if she were still a virgin. She didn't answer. Her worst problem seemed to be that she was twenty-nine and sexually untouched. He put all the tenderness he could command into his voice. He wanted to help, not hurt her further. Problems mattered less than one's reaction to them. Confidence bred further confidence. She had been so much help to him, now, let him help her. She was valuable, the most valuable person at the Centre. She whispered that she lived for art. And animals, of course.

'I know. I do too.'

If that were only true. It used to be true. At this present moment he lived to get her into her sleeping bag. He drew her head gently to him. There now, rest on his shoulder, he was reliable, he'd never let her down. He took her in his arms, tenderly wiping her eyes. The left one looked at his face, the other across his shoulder. In truth they were pretty eyes. He stroked with his left hand, moving down over her skin, through the loose neck of her jersey. Her breasts were like small ears, stiffening when he touched. She was still trembling, her breathing came in pants. A small animal, a pretty creature, he'd tame her with kindness and skill. How fond he could become of her. They belonged, she must feel it too. Off with that vest and those uncomfortable jeans. Carefully, mustn't snag the zip. Lovely little stomach, so white, so soft, such furry bushy hair. She might be a virgin but she was far from frigid, she was as warm as fire. Ease the left hand into those creases, so wet and welcoming. Fran. Oh Fran.

'Eric. No. Eric.'

'I'm not going to do anything you don't want. You know that. Now, what about those socks?'

The left one first, peel it down delicately. Long white toes, a lovely foot. Now the right sock, gently, mustn't stare. Five toes, all present, narrow and white like the left. But the heel, where was her heel? A web of tendons and puckered muscle tissue was attached to her ankle bone, a sort of hard sponge, not a heel. He smoothed it wonderingly, poor heel, it wasn't as bad as his hand. And no one saw it, it was hidden under a sock and shoe. The whole world saw his hand. See, look, her foot fitted his hand, made to join, a single shape, rather beautiful. No more tears or fears, no more feelings of being a freak. She was lovely, she must believe that.

'The fire's dying, Eric.'

'I'll warm you. Let me look after you.'

'I'm afraid.'

'No need. I'm here. Come.'

Deep into the sleeping bag with him, nothing to frighten her at all. He'd be responsible, leave everything to him. Huge erection, deep in the bag, dark, warm, wet. What buttocks she had, what hair, she didn't seem virgin at all.

'What's that noise? Stop, Eric.'

'You smell glorious, so natural. Don't worry about a noise.'

'Wait. There it is. Listen.'

'It's just squirrels. Or the birds in the chimney. They're noisiest at night.'

'That's not birds, it's too loud. Birds don't sound like that. There.'

'They're pushing rubbish down, that's all. The fire is out, it must be a rubbish fall.'

There came a slithering crash in the fireplace, something was in the hearth. Not leaves or dead twigs or nutshells, something alive with them. Something fourlegged was scuttling in the cabin. Fran struggled out of the sleeping bag. She screamed. It was the cat, the one they'd lost when the hens went, it was their cat, the one called Babe.

'Fran, leave it alone. Ignore it. Come back here to me.'

'Babe. Here, Babe, my honey. To me, Babe, to me.'

He shouted at her, he tried begging, the animal was too wild. She'd get cold out of bed, come back at once. He heard the typewriter crash. Then the hotplate clattered, the pan was knocked over, something raced over the boards. It was on the sleeping bag, he felt claws touching him, then it had run down inside. Fran come here, it was on him. He couldn't undo the zip. The zip caught in his pyjama coat. Help, Fran. Come here. He felt teeth biting, something wet. Something . . .

'I'm coming, Babe, it's all right, hon. Babe . . . Jesus Chr – ist. It's not Babe. It's . . . oh Eric. Oh Jeeesus Chr – ist.'

He was bleeding, he was in pain, he smelled foul. He felt for the switch in the dark.

Fran was crouched by the pallet. Jesus. The animal was still in the bag. They heard it hissing and spitting, the lump was halfway down. No cat made sounds like that, not even an American one. She pulled the zip down slowly, she pulled the bag away. A small black and white beast growled at them, a beast with a bushy tail. There was an unearthly stink, worse than sewer gas, more pungent than ammonia or rotting garlic. His eyes streamed, he tried not to retch. They put their clothing on. Fran was sobbing. The beast ran across to the fire.

They went outside into the snow again, they breathed the clean cold air. Skunk oil was ineradicable, Fran told him. The cabin would have to be closed. Anything touched by a skunk had to be burned or destroyed. Tomato juice would neutralize the smell on their bodies, they'd get rid of the smell on themselves, though it would take time. Everything else must be incinerated, all papers, clothing, books. It was the finish of his work at Penn Center and the finish of his friendship with Fran.

CHAPTER ELEVEN

Ivy

'Your Dad and I can't do everything always, Vee. You've turned into yourself too much. There's your future to think about. You can't stop in bed with that cat always.'

Vee was getting worse. This break in Shadwell wasn't helping her. She lay around complaining of sickness every morning, she wouldn't discuss the child. She kept staring into a mirror, saying she wanted to go back to Spain.

'I couldn't go away, Vee, I couldn't leave your Dad. Besides, isn't Eric due home soon? Have you forgotten him?'

'He forgot me, didn't he? Besides, I need a break. I never asked for all this.'

'Don't you know where Eric is stopping? Funny he never wrote.'

'He did give the address to me. I lost it. He never bothered, why should I? He just went off, as you know.'

'What will you do next, Vee? Where will you live when it's born?'

'Don't start pestering again. I haven't decided. I'll very likely go for a divorce.'

'You can't. You mustn't. You're a . . . Oh my lor'.'

'Don't start that religious stuff, Ivy. I want to go back to Spain.'

She was like a baby; if she wanted anything she had to have it at once. Ches said not to fuss her, let her decide herself. But there was a grandchild to think of, wasn't there. A kiddy needed two parents and a home with love and warmth. She chewed at her cheek, she felt anxious. Such a long cold spring they'd had, no end to the ice and sleet. She'd read about the snow blizzards in America; they were getting what the Yanks had here. She'd thought she'd seen some snowdrops yesterday, but it was just some torn bus tickets and stuff. What was wrong with Vee? She took no exercise, didn't even play records no more or wear jewellery. Her hair was its normal shade, that was something, but her eyes looked all miserable and forlorn.

She was pleased when Charmian got in touch with them, she was that worried about Vee. She rang to say that Eric was stopping on longer in America, because of pressure of work. And would Ivy tell Violet please? Ruddy cheek. Why couldn't Eric tell Vee himself? What was up with him?

'Oh, come on, Charmian,' she'd said to her. 'You can tell me, what's it about? Is Eric ill or what?' She felt sorry for Charmian really, she guessed she was feeling ashamed. The way she felt ashamed of Vee sometimes. Eric was like Vee, the way he relied on his Mum. Children showed you up, big or little. When they were little your arms ached, your heart ached when they got big. He must get his selfishness from Charmian. Never would she forget the way she'd crept out of the church, with that stuck-up look on her face, nor would she forget the way she'd gone for Vee that time, in Vee's own house too. Now she was getting paid back, having to pass Eric's messages on. Still, no sense in holding a grudge. So she rang Charmian back.

'Now look, Charmian, you must know more about Eric than you're letting on. Come on, I'm your friend.'

'I appreciate your amicability, Ivy. I'm slightly concerned, I admit. Not worried, you understand, just mildly concerned. I assure you I know nothing. He's not written to me either. His project evidently demands all his time.'

'Oh yes, Vee said. His play. We thought he'd gone

teaching.'

Eric was a clever man, granted. The Stubbs lot weren't too fond of plays. She and Ches went more for spectaculars. 'Course, Eric and Charmian never watched the telly, so what could you expect? As a family they were quite cagey. The Stubbs didn't believe in secrets. How long did play-writing take? She'd bet Eric had another woman.

'Tell me . . . how is Violet?'

'I was wondering when you'd ask. She's gone all quiet. She's changed since the start of all this.'

About time the Lady C showed some interest. She had a heart in her somewhere. They ought to manage to be friends.

'I would like to extend the olive branch. I'd like to invite you and Violet to tea. How would Thursday suit you both? Please, Ivy, do say yes.'

'Pardon, dear?'

'Our last meeting could hardly be called auspicious. I would like to make amends.'

'Tea? Vee and me? Very well, I'll ask her.'

She would relish a chance to take a look at that 'Purple Rest' again, to check on what else the Lady C had been getting up to. It must have taken some nerve to do what she'd done, pulling the place apart. Granted it had too much purple, and far too many ornaments. It was a matter of choice, she could see both sides to the question. Life couldn't have been easy for Charm, without a proper man to love or to love her, only that son of hers who had that funny hand. She'd spoiled him rotten, she could understand that too. 'Course, the antique world had class. She'd be surprised though if Vee would want to have tea there, not after that fuss last time. At the present moment the girl didn't know what she wanted, excepting to go back to Spain.

She was wrong though, Vee was keen.

'If Eric can stop in America, you and I can go to Spain. We'll go and have tea with Charmian, we'll take Dick along too. He

101

can stay there while we're away. Then Dad won't have to look after him. Dick belongs there, it's his house. Charmian can lump it.'

It seemed rude to turn up with a cat. It made Ivy feel awkward. Still, the whole situation was awkward, not knowing who belonged where.

The bus put them down at the corner of the green. Ivy looked across at the snowy grass. There was the corner house, all white now behind the snow. Ever so pure looking, reminded her of Violet as she was once. Now she only cared for her cat, who'd played them up something rotten on the way here. She wondered if the Lady C was looking out for them, behind that double glaze.

The inner door clicked, there she was, in pale grey knitted silk.

'Hey, Vee, don't let the cat go yet. Wait till we get inside.'

They grabbed. They shouted. His thin tail slipped through Ivy's hand. He streaked round the side of the house.

'A cat? I wasn't expecting . . . I wish you had asked me first.'

'I told Vee she ought to, she wouldn't take a bit of notice.'

'Dick. My poor little cat.'

'He'll be back, don't you worry, Vee. This is where he lives.'

'Not now it isn't. Not after what she done to the place. He won't know it without me there. Dick . . . Dick.'

'You should have thought of that. You would bring him.'

'Now, Violet, I agree with your mother. There's no need to dramatize. He'll come back.'

'We don't want your advice. You spoiled everything.'

'Shame, Vee, don't be so rude. Don't take no notice of her, Charmian, the girl isn't herself.'

She tried to explain about the holiday, that she and Vee were going away, that was why Vee brought her cat. She ought to have asked, it was naughty. But Chester had allergies with cats. That was at the back of this, Chester's rash.

'But . . . Ivy . . . I have to tell you. I'm not fond of cats myself. I have total sympathy with Chester.'

'You see, Vee? I told you.'

'And apart from that, is a holiday quite prudent at this particular time? Did you consult your practitioner, Violet?'

'My what? Eric's away, isn't he? I'll sodding do as I please. This is my house, Charmian, remember, until I decide to leave. So don't get carried away.'

Ivy felt red with shame at the way Vee spoke to Charm. The woman was trying to be matey. Vee could be diabolical when she wanted. She didn't want 'Purple Rest', least she didn't appear to. And Charm had done it up nice inside. All that white and grey had a lot more class than Vee's purple, it looked a lot more genteel. And Charm, with her white hair and grey silk, looked nice here. Excepting for Vee they all hated cats, that was the trouble.

'Those look nice, Charm, dear.'

At the Buildings they usually ate sliced white from a packet. Brown bread with seeds made a change. And honey in the comb. Vee might as well stop worrying about Dick and sit down to a lovely tea. She was out there by the back door shouting for him. The cat would come when it chose. The bar looked ever so nice as a dining-room, with a nice mahogany table for tea. She didn't miss Vee's guns and piano. She liked the water-coloured pictures on the wall, and those grey curtains. Restful, that was the word, and pretty too.

'I'm delighted that you approve the change, Ivy. I'm just doing as I was asked.'

'I'm still interested to know what he's up to. But you have improved the place. It's got something it didn't have with Vee in it. 'Course, she's young. Kids like to whatsername . . . experiment. She's not quite herself just now.'

'I suppose that's understandable.'

'I worry just the same. She won't talk a word about the baby. She's unnatural, to my way of thought.'

'She will. She'll adjust. We'll start tea, shall we?'

'You're kind, Charmian, I must say, more understanding than I thought. Are *you* pleased about the child?'

She'd surprised Charmian by asking her outright, she wasn't used to plain speaking, her kind never were. But Charmian wasn't as bad as some of them, all 'how-now' and no heart. Underneath she was probably all right. Come on now, say, was she pleased?

'At first . . . I was . . . taken aback, Ivy. Well . . . appalled, I have to admit.'

'I knew it. I guessed. But now?'

'We must accept life. New birth. Growth. You might find that after your holiday Violet is completely changed. She will mature, I am sure of it. You must use your own judgement of course, but I don't think you have cause for concern. Go on the holiday, enjoy it. The cat will be safe here.'

'Charm, that is kind, really. I was for that marriage as you know.'

She told her that she'd started knitting. Privately she wasn't at all sure about Eric, not now. Why *was* he stopping away? He didn't appear to appreciate Vee. And after all her strictness, keeping her fresh as cream. Charmian repeated that she was at a loss, mystified about Eric's absence. The whole episode had caused her to think.

'About what, Charm dear?'

'About Eric and Violet. A child could be the answer. A child consolidates a union.'

'That's what I think. There's two sides to every question. My Vee's not perfect. She can be lazy, she can be rude. Here she is now again. Come on, Vee. Any sign of the cat?'

'If he's disappeared I'll never forgive myself.'

'He'll turn up again. Cats do. See the tea Charmian's laid on for us. Honey in the comb.'

'I can't eat brown bread. Is that tea strong?'

'I apologize Violet. It is China tea I'm afraid.'

'Might have known. I won't have anything. Dick will need a

lot of milk. If he comes back.'

'Vee, stop it. Charm's doing all she can. Can't you be civil? Charm's started knitting too.'

'I didn't ask her to. You'll be expecting me to knit next.'

'Well, seeing it's your child . . .'

'All those pink and blue woollies. Dead boring. You can stuff them. Oh all right, I'll have some cake.'

'Not white woollens? Don't you like white? A newly-born infant looks adorable in white. When Eric was . . .'

'I don't want to hear about him. I hate pinks and blues and whites. I don't like woollies at all. Our child will be born modern.'

Ivy hoped Charmian would understand Vee's attitude. Pregnancy had made her strange. She wanted to hear a lot more about Charmian's life. They had things in common after all. Poor woman, she was managing best way she could. She probably missed Eric a lot, plus his father who was dead. Antiques were a nice line to be in. She wanted to learn about that. She'd like to see Charm's tapestry.

CHAPTER TWELVE

Violet

The best part about going away was leaving the awful cold.
The cold didn't used to bother her. It was when she got
married she started noticing it. Inside the Buildings seemed
colder than outside; the only warm place was in bed. She knew
she complained. It was mean really, 'cos they loved her.
They'd put up with Dick as well. Only she felt so sick now, not
just mornings, daytime as well. Her mouth went full of spit,
she kept yawning, everything tasted bad. She missed the
radiators, the double glazing and carpets. She didn't see herself
going back to 'Purple Rest', not after what Charmian had
done. At the Buildings there was just cold linoleum that Ivy
polished, and scatter rugs that slipped. There wasn't proper
hot water, you had to run the geyser before it got warm. The
bathroom was as cold as a fridge because Dad believed in a
simple life. Because he worked in the open he thought
everyone ought to be tough. Most people had their funny
ideas, with Ivy it was sex. She'd been funny about keeping her
fresh for marriage, as she called it. As if anyone was these days.
Ivy had pushed her into Eric's arms before she'd known
anything. Now look at her. She didn't want Eric, or a baby.
She would most probably get a divorce.

Ivy had always pushed her around, she was half afraid of her
still. It seemed like all her life she'd been listening to her. Ivy
talking, telling her what was right and what wasn't. Ivy
making those noises, in the night, animal noises, grunting

noises behind their bedroom door. 'Aagh. Aaagh. Don't. We mustn't let Vee hear.' She had heard and she'd hated it. She used to put her ear to the keyhole, very excited. Scared. What did they do in there? What was the secret? She used to go back to bed, pull up the blankets, worry about them. Imagine things. It was after that first time that she'd started having her dream. Sometimes she had it still, not often. A huge hand would appear in the black sky over her like a painting dotted with lights. The dream wasn't frightening. One reason she'd wanted to leave home was to get away from those noises. Ivy wanted her to change, be like Eric, go up in the world. Eric did nothing but criticize. They both wanted her different. Eric would sooner have his mother. Not on the honeymoon. They had been happy then. On honeymoon she'd liked his hand. He'd known how to love her, she was his delight, his wonder. 'I love you, I want you, you're mine.' Their hotel was the biggest, their room like a bridal suite. Nothing was too good for her then, she could have anything she liked. She could do anything she liked with the house, make changes, buy anything. The house was hers too. Remember? As mistress she should feel free. He was a liar, he hadn't meant it. Now he had flown away. She had expected him to come after her, beg her to leave Shadwell, come back. Instead he'd flown away and stayed away. Well, now she was flying too. On holiday with Ivy, going to Spain. The same town, same hotel, without him. She'd wipe out the memory of that honeymoon. She'd sooner have Ivy now.

'Vee, have we left the ground yet? I'm scared. Have we started?'

'You're daft, Ivy. We're flying now. We're in the air. Open your eyes.'

Since she'd said goodbye to Dad, Ivy had lost confidence. Too afraid to look at the sky out there, all blue with clouds like wool. The bluest sky ever. Eric used to call her eyes 'rinsed blue'. That was a long time ago, before she became trollop and cur.

'Open your eyes, Ivy, do.'

But she sat clutching her arm rests, her chin all shapeless with fear. Ivy worried about leaving Dad, in case he got poorly. She worried about going by air. Dick was all right, he'd turned up, as Charmian said he would. They'd have some fun in Spain.

'My head hurts, Vee. It's my ears.'

'Undo the seat belt now. Your ears will stop soon. It's pressure. Going up and coming down.'

'You sure?'

''Course. Eric told me. They'll bring round drinks soon. And snacks too. You can buy things on the plane.'

'What? Perfume?'

'If you want. And pens. Sometimes they have silk scarves.'

She'd gone off perfume since this baby business, she didn't even like violets now. So far she'd seen to all the arrangements, the luggage, the tickets and that. She wished Ivy would stop looking so half-baked. Once at Gatwick she'd gone like a child.

'Watch the hostess, Ivy, she's showing us what to do. Watch her with the life jacket.'

'Why? What's she doing that for?'

'Case we crash, 'course.'

'Oh Vee. I can't.'

Violet stared at her. She'd never seen Ivy like this. Because her feet weren't on land she'd gone all ugly and old. A bit different from what she'd been in the night. At it again, she'd heard them. 'Aagh. Don't. We mustn't let Vee hear.' At their age. Disgusting. Dad must go without it now for a week.

'Ivy, you look awful. Do open your eyes.'

'Are your ears giving trouble, madam? Please let me help.'

'It's okay. My Mum isn't used to flying. I'll see to her.'

She wouldn't fancy earning her living in the sky, wouldn't fancy having to bother with passengers like Ivy. They took the girls with posh accents for that job anyway. Ivy was making a

108

silly fuss. If you swallowed it went away.

'Look, Ivy. Pepsis.'

They loved fizzy drinks with straws. Cream soda was Violet's favourite, you could drink a lot without feeling sick. She hoped that Ivy would stop looking all daft and sweaty by the time they got to Spain. Her blouse buttons were undone, her shoes were too tight. She didn't want to worry about Ivy or her ears, she wanted to think about Spain. She wanted to be first off the plane and feel that sun again. She put on her dark glasses.

She stood at the top of the gangway, she felt the heat on her head. Between her thighs and under her arms she felt prickly. Lovely to feel the sweat. She tilted her face back. Heat, colours, smells, all here, just the same. There were the brown-necked men, short mostly, their black hair as shiny as shoes. They called to each other unsmilingly. When they saw her their narrow eyes looked bold. They handled luggage, checked landing cards, stamped passports, their brown hands ringed with gold. Their cigarette smell wasn't like English smoke, there was creosote in it, and sweat. Outside the airport somewhere there was a tenor voice and a guitar.

'Hurry, Ivy. You can put your passport away now.'

Ivy still looked silly and old. Their courier, a blonde woman called Diamond who stood by the waiting coach, looked at her, helping her up the steps. Diamond sat by the driver shouting information in different languages. But Ivy only closed her eyes again. She'd seen nothing of the flight, she was missing their first sight of Spain. The blue skies, bright foliage and music might as well be London for all Ivy seemed to care.

Violet looked at the palm trees, the giant cactus plants, the bougainvillaea bordering the dusty streets. People wearing sun dresses or bikinis idled past the shops on their way to the beach. They sat at tables outside cafés eating ices or drinking coffee. The ices were layered and elaborate, with coloured jelly and fruit. The drinks came in tall straight glasses coloured yellow,

109

red and green. The Spanish took their business seriously, they knew the best ways to please. Older Spanish women with tired faces carried shopping from the market. The lightly clad holiday-makers carried sun oil and cameras, kicking off their sandals under the café tables. Diamond shouted the town's attractions. Still Ivy wouldn't look. Each time they paused at traffic lights, Diamond explained the route. She conducted her passengers into the various hotels. They passed a shopping arcade.

'Look, Ivy. Clothes.'

Trays of shoes, gloves, leather hats were laid out to tempt passers by. Plastic toys were slung over broomsticks. Rosary beads were looped round plaster statues and over the corners of holy pictures. Inlaid steel-backed handmirrors and knives with intricate handles glittered in the hard light. There were paperweights with little animals in them, all objects to charm the heart. Chemists' windows displayed talcum powder and boxes of marbled soap. She remembered that soap, many-coloured, containing iodine and glycerine. She sighed. She was breathing in Spain again. She could smell charcoal, cooking oil, garlic, the fishy salt of the sea. They caught glimpses of the beach between the breaks in the skyscrapers and shops. Birds twittered from cages in apartment windows and flowers grew everywhere. There were hanging baskets, tubs, flower beds and banks of flowering shrubs. Stray dogs on corners stared at lurking ill-fed cats. A church clock chimed.

'Hotel Excelsior,' said Diamond.

They turned into a courtyard. More banks of flowers, more plate-glass windows, stretches of shining chrome. A great awning stretched over the doorway.

'Look, Ivy. Wake up now. We're here.'

'Vee. It's a mammoth place. You never said.'

'I said it was posh. Four star.'

As she got down from the coach Ivy stumbled. So large a place, could it really be theirs for a week? Violet felt like

110

pinching her. They'd paid, hadn't they? Got their booking? The stout German couple standing behind them rolled their eyes meaningfully. 'Mein Gott. Englishers.'

Violet explained to Ivy that they must get the room key first. Ivy wasn't used to hotels. She still looked half daft, fumbling at her blouse. The Germans pushed in front with their strong continental luggage, breathing heavily in the backs of their noses. The four of them went up in the lift together. The Germans' fat necks were reflected in the steel doors. Their suite adjoined Violet's and Ivy's.

'Now, Ivy. We've got the very same room. In here.'

'Same as what?'

'The one I was in before.'

Ivy suddenly changed. The sight of luxury and quiet restored her. She sat on the bed near the door. She stroked it. So comfy and soft and wide. Flowers too, they'd put flowers in vases as if they were royalty. The dark solid furniture against the white and gold walls went a treat with them yellow curtains. She liked everything she saw.

'Glad you do. And the bathroom. In here, look.'

She watched Ivy touching the bidet taps with a churchy look on her face. Watched her turn the hot tap on. Really hot. At once. Watched her fingering the soap. Plenty of towels and toilet paper. The room was a dream come true.

'We got a fridge too. Here by the door. For snacks or fizzy drinks.'

Eric had put champagne in that fridge, with grapes and sprays of flowers. He'd bought her liqueur chocolates and lobster, shown her the haute cuisine. He'd never change her. For her it was a bun and chip life, while he chose cheeses and hare.

Ivy switched the lights on and off, there were wall lights, two chandeliers and lamps. There was air-conditioning, radio and television. She wanted to stop for life. Double doors led on to a covered balcony with a cane table and a swinging chair.

111

Violet sat on the chair again. She and Eric had swung here and kissed. You could lean on the wall of the balcony to watch the people below. Sunbathers lay in rows on the sand or splashed in and out of the sea. She didn't like getting sunburned and Eric didn't like showing his hand. They'd spent a lot of time on this balcony. There were the pedal boats that you could hire, from the man with the leather bag. There were the pleasure boats taking trips around the bay. Ivy leaned over, delighted. The wall of the balcony had leafy plants growing along the top. The bricks were hot under your skin. Just what they needed, a balcony, Ivy said. She would buy a washing line.

'What for?'

'So we can wash our clothes.'

'Don't be daft, Ivy. That isn't suitable. People don't wash their clothes here.'

Trust her to want to start scrubbing and rubbing before they'd barely arrived. She'd no idea how to behave. She was only used to caravans. Looked as if she'd have to show her everything. When she'd seen the fridge she'd wanted to rush out for some sandwiches. She didn't know what a siesta was.

'You can watch the telly, Ivy, if you don't fancy sleeping now. We'll go shopping later, after dinner. They stay open late in Spain.'

Ivy switched on the set and sat down on her bed.

'A bullfight, Vee. Look, how cruel.'

There was the yellow sand again, the blood of the dark coloured bulls. There was the matador, the toreador, the picadors, Eric had explained it all. The glitter and gloss was exciting, it wasn't cruel in Spain. This place was different to England, they made killing a work of art, working off their feelings against animals.

Ivy said what was good about bulls bleeding, what was artistic about those knives? They were needed for food, Eric had told her, they had to die anyway, they would end as pieces

112

of steak. Ivy stared. What did Vee mean exactly? What was the need for steak? They both disliked meat, except for sausages sometimes. Was Vee saying bullfighting was right?

Violet didn't think it was right, she'd felt like crying when she first saw it, from that bed where Ivy was sitting. On that very spot they had kissed and made love.

Though Ivy was happy now she was still different. As though she was the child and Violet the mother now. She had to have everything explained, had to be shown how to behave. Spain was lovely still, she didn't feel sick any more, didn't feel she had a baby in her now.

Ivy put on a flimsy frock later, which didn't suit her at all.

'But I thought you'd like it, Vee.'

'Well I don't. It's cut too low for Spain. Your perfume is too strong.'

She watched Ivy's face. She liked hurting her. She wanted to get back at her for all the times she'd bossed, all the times she'd scared her with those night noises. She knew more than Ivy now, she was travelled, she knew how to act in Spain. Ivy looked like a Christmas tree with her beads and perfume and frills.

As they went out on to the landing the German couple came out. They had both changed into grey clothes. A linen suit for her, grey cotton pinstripe for him. They bowed their iron grey heads without speaking, proceeding to the lift.

Leaving their suite made Ivy shy again. She didn't speak inside the lift. Their suite was their hideaway, the hotel was so posh. They walked across areas of deep carpeting, past low tables and chairs where the guests smoked and sipped cocktails. Violet said they wouldn't wait, they'd go straight to the dining-room, find out where they would be sitting. The waiter showed them to the first window bay, here was their table for the week. His hair smelled of roses and onions as he pulled out Ivy's chair. She looked thrilled. Violet shrugged. It took more than a smile to impress her, or a lick of hair oil. She wasn't nervous, she'd sat at this table before. The waiter offered Ivy the wine list, giving a saucy wink.

'This is my first time in Spain, dear. You'll have to excuse my ignorance. Which wine would *you* think best?'

'Some little bubbly, madam? Drink to the happy day? Champagne on ice?'

'Oooh. Shall we, Vee? Champagne on the Costa del Sol? You see, dear, this is my daughter. She's been here before. Lovely girl, isn't she?'

'As beautiful as her mother, madam.'

Ivy explained that it was Vee's idea to come. She'd stayed in this very part of Spain, same hotel, same rooms. Coincidence wasn't it?

'Don't tell him all that, Ivy. It's embarrassing. He doesn't want to hear.'

'Why be shy about it, Vee. It's the truth isn't it? And . . . dear? Guess what next. Vee has a secret this time, a special one. Can you guess what it is?'

'Stop it, Ivy. Shut your mouth.'

'Don't be so rude, Vee. People will hear.'

'It's you what's doing the shouting. Why don't you keep quiet?'

At the next table the German couple rolled their eyes again, their hands stayed still over their plates. Ivy looked boldly at them, then she looked at the wine waiter. Vee's secret was inside her. Her condition was delicate. Get the picture?

'Shut up, Ivy. You cow.'

She hated them all. She hated Ivy. She hated the hotel in Spain. She should have come back here alone. Ivy had made her a show.

When Eric and she sat at this table overlooking that dark sea, and watched that same sky, nearly black now, just streaked with green, he'd given her titbits, had touched her, had refilled her glass with wine. She'd touched his hand, thought she loved him. Did love usually melt like smoke? He'd bought her perfumes which she'd spilled and forgotten. He'd bought her silky things embroidered with flowers. He'd told her their love would last if they kept the purse filled. He'd filled her with kisses, into her mouth, between her legs, on her buttocks. His wife and his love, remember? 'I need you, I want you, you're mine.' Where was that purse now? What had happened to it? Not that it mattered any more.

The green streaks in the sky faded. All was blackness. There'd be stars there when your eyes got accustomed. Ivy watched the waiter's hair. She spoke of the flight coming over, her ears hurt her, she'd been strapped in. Air travel was all right once you got used to it. And that Diamond had been there when they got down. She was looking forward to seeing the town later and the things Diamond had spoken about.

'Shut up, Ivy. They know. They all came here the same way.'

'Now pardon me, Vee, let me speak. The Germans are keen to be friends, anyway. Whatever about the others.'

'Can't we keep to ourselves? We don't have to get involved do we? Not at first, at any rate.'

Ivy said that part of getting away was making friends. It wasn't only the change, you met new people. That wine waiter was quite pally.

'Oh hello, dear, I was just talking about you, just saying how friendly you were. What do you think of my dress? My daughter says it's too young.'

'Ivy.'

'Beautiful, madam. For you nothing is too young.'

'Between you and me and the wall she's just jealous. You get funny ideas with the first.'

There was no stopping Ivy. She was doing it on purpose to get attention for herself. She wanted everyone in the dining-room to watch her, especially that wine waiter. Ivy was the jealous one, she wished she was dead. She held her knife and fork wrong, she chewed in a horrible way. When she wasn't eating she chewed her cheek. She smelled like a scent factory. She showed off too much bust. The waiter couldn't take his eyes off her; everyone knew what Spaniards were like. He was half Ivy's age too – disgusting. Look at him now, offering Ivy pistachio ice cream with nuts in, peering down her dress.

'Okay, dear, I'll have a portion. Vee, if you don't want some you should go to bed early. You're looking quite poorly again.'

CHAPTER THIRTEEN

Violet

She jumped. She must have been nearly asleep. She forgot
where she was until she smelled the hotel. The furniture polish,
laundry starch, soap, the dryness of conditioned air. The fridge
clicked behind her, in the distance a dog howled. She was
standing on the veranda looking over the sea again. Her eyelids
must have closed because she'd seen that dream hand again,
bigger, brighter than ever, picked out in lights over her head.
The dog's howls had woken her. She looked up. No hand any
more. The sky was empty but for a few pale stars.

She had come up here again without Ivy. After the pistachio
ice and their coffee they had gone to the boutique in the foyer
and Ivy had seen the dress. It beckoned her from among the
bags and shoes, a purple lurex tunic with a bead fringe and
braid. It was too tight on her; she wanted it. And those purple
shoes to match. She explained to the assistant that her daughter
criticized her, had said that she didn't look right for Spain.
She'd like to buy this shiny number with the bead neck-strap
that kept it up. It cut into her a bit, no matter, it was worth it to
look so nice. Violet had said that it was brighter and tighter
than the dress she'd been wearing. Ivy laughed and bought a
watch too, a crystal ball on a chain. Violet would have worn
clothes like that when she was home. On Ivy they looked a
show. She had asked for her pink dress to be wrapped. She
would keep the beady one on while they went to the cocktail
lounge. The German couple passed the boutique. Ivy shouted

117

after them.

'Hey, you two. We sleep next to your room. How do you like this gown?'

They bowed their iron grey heads but didn't reply. Ivy turned back to the mirror, settling the beading again. Her neck looked sore already, her bottom bulged under her skirt. She needed a champagne cocktail now, to chase that dinner down.

She put a leg up on the bar stool, her veined thigh showed through the beads. She watched herself in the bar mirror. Then the wine waiter came to work his shift in the cocktail lounge. Yes, madam – champagne cocktail, speciality of the Excelsior. Violet had a Pepsi. Of course Ivy wanted her youth, it was natural. She'd not been abroad before. If only she'd stop chewing her cheek and rubbing that beaded strap. Her eyes went daft when she spoke to the waiter. This Pepsi tasted sharper than the kind at home. Where was home, her real home? She didn't want to live at the Buildings any more and they didn't want her there. Had she lost 'Purple Rest'? She and the baby would have to live somewhere. Idle wishing didn't help. She left Ivy and the wine waiter without them noticing. Her dark dress and dark glasses were too quiet for the cocktail lounge. She'd go up and look at the stars.

The brickwork in the veranda was warm still though the air was cooler now, with the stuffy cool that comes before another hot day. She leaned against the wall. The small plants rasped her arms, the stalks tickled. She looked out at the sea. The starlight and the lights from the fishing boats blended. She wondered about the hand in the sky. It had looked so real. It must have been a dream. Eric had once said that dreams that kept recurring had a special meaning; the things you most needed were trying to make themselves known. The imagination never slept. What did she need? She didn't like being married or being pregnant. Why did she feel so discontented? Why a lit-up hand? She and Eric had made love on this veranda, had put cushions down on the tiles. Afterwards they used to lie listening to the waves out there and dogs barking. She had learned about physical love here. There was more to loving than sex.

She heard a sound in the bedroom behind her. Ivy was back, full of champagne and flattery. Someone was moving behind the frosted glass of the bathroom door. Someone laughed. Someone turned a tap.

'What time is it, Ivy? Who's with you in there?'

She came out. Her feet were bare, the strap of her bra was loose, her crimson mouth looked smudged. She held two glasses. The wine waiter came out after her, a bottle in his hand.

'A little nightcap, Vee. We thought you'd like one. I didn't like to think of you alone up here, on your first night abroad. This is my friend Jose.'

'I've been standing outside on the veranda. You know I don't drink champagne. I'm not supposed to have alcohol now.'

Jose was dapper as ever, each polished hair in place. His shirt sleeves were rolled neatly. He'd removed his bow tie. He looked at her.

'Hundred apologies, beautiful madam. Your mother asked. Some little bubbly?'

'I don't want it. You can go now, Jose. Thanks.'

'That's rude, Vee. Jose has been ever so kind. Whoops, Jo, don't spill any. My Vee's in the family way.'

'Take it away. I don't want any. Get out.'

'Oh, be like that then. Come on, Jo. There's no fun in here, let's go on the veranda.'

They closed the double doors, leaving her in the bedroom. Alone, excluded. Left out. The television screen was blank when she switched it on. The hotel was quiet, the guests were asleep. She put her ear to the door handle, she held her breath. 'Aagh. Aaagh. Don't. We mustn't let Vee hear.'

How could Ivy? Disgusting. A sin.

'Stop it. Stop, Ivy.'

'Don't be like that, Vee. Oh my lor! It's just a bit of fun.'

'Fun you call it? Look, Jose, that's my mother. Let her alone.'

'Go away. Don't annoy us, Vee. Just because you . . .'

Under the light of the veranda Ivy lay on the tiles. A cushion was arranged under her, her knickers hung over the chair. Violet felt the scattered beads from the new dress pricking the soles of her feet. Jose looked sheepish. He smoothed his polished hair.

'How dare you. Leave my mother alone.'

'Beautiful madam. I meant no harm. The lady asked.'

'Leave her. Go away.'

'I come to Excelsior recently. My job is to be nice. If customers ask, if they wish . . .'

'Shut your mouth. Go away.'

She felt his hand on her arm, trying to persuade her, stroking her, rubbing her wrist. If he touched any more she'd be sick. A dog howled across the bay. Eric, where are you? Why did you go away? I need you. The same veranda, same cushion, same tiles.

He was whispering something.

'I'll ring for the manager. Sod off.'

'That's very rude indeed, Vee. Don't take no notice, Jo.'

'This is my trip. I suggested coming here. You just do what I say and shut your mouth, Ivy.'

Jose took a comb from his hip pocket, ran it through his hair. He rolled his sleeves down. Before he put his coat on he clipped his bow tie into place. He put on the coat and left.

Ivy looked at her, with eyes like a naughty child. Violet hit her, on her mouth and across her neck. She saw that smeared lipstick and hit it. This was power, she was hurting at last. The Stubbs family never went in for violence, she'd never been bashed in her life. She was a Caive-Propp, behaving like Charmian. She was hitting and couldn't stop.

'Why, Ivy? Why did you do that? Why?'

'Whatever have we done to each other? Why do you hate me? I'm your Mum.'

'Because everything's your fault. Everything's wrong because of you.'

Because of Ivy she'd married too young, before knowing what Eric was like. Because of Ivy's religious ideas she'd had nothing to do with boys. She'd not known any, she'd not known about sex. She'd got this baby in her because she'd not known what to do. Ivy's religion again. She wanted to hit her till she killed her, hit her till her arm dropped off. Ivy didn't resist, didn't avoid her, just stood in her torn frock and bare feet. At last she stopped.

'Don't you love me no more, Vee? Don't you even love your Dad?'

'Dad? How can you speak about him? Your husband. I've heard you with him. Night after night. And now that . . . waiter. Like animals, you and he. I heard.'

'I love your Dad, Vee. You know I do. He's my world.'

'Your world? What kind of a world when you . . . That waiter. Ugh.'

'You've no need to act so holy, Vee. You're not perfect, nor am I. I was just fooling, just a bit of fun. I love Ches, you know I do.'

'A funny way to show it. You and that waiter.'

'You were acting so high and mighty. As if you were ashamed of me. I was lonely.'

'Lonely? What about my Dad?'

'Well he isn't your Dad if you want to know. There. I've told you now.'

'Not? What did you say?'

'Ches isn't your real Dad, not your blood father. No one knows, not even him. I was going to tell you sometime. It might as well be now.'

'Who is then? Who was it? Who is my father?'

'I married Ches before you got born. You ain't a bastard, Vee.'

'Who? Who?'

'I don't know. One night. Ches was away. Someone I met at the *palais de danse*, actually, same place as I met Ches. It happened before we got married.'

Violet looked at her. She felt tired and very sick again. Ivy wasn't what she made out to be, she'd not been a virgin bride herself. Wasn't even faithful to Dad. She wished she'd not found out, wished she hadn't hit her. It hadn't helped, it made everything worse. The dog howled again. Ivy said that it was funny that none of them liked dogs when they were supposed to be such faithful animals.

CHAPTER FOURTEEN

Violet

She had shouted at Ivy to tell her. She must remember. Who? Who was that man at the *palais*? What had he been like? Did Ivy realize what she'd done to her? She had taken her roots away. As if having this baby wasn't enough, now she didn't feel sure of anything, didn't know who she was. Who was the man?

She saw now why she didn't look like Chester. How could she trust Ivy now? She'd made a fool out of Dad. That waiter, young enough to be her son. Who else had there been? How many? Had she married Dad for a roof? Ivy shook her head, silly tears in her eyes.

'I don't know. We just met the once. Don't shout, Vee, the Germans will hear.'

She hoped they would hear, she hoped the whole hotel would hear. This whole trip had been a mistake. If only she'd brought her Dad. Why had Ivy insisted on purity when she'd been no virgin herself?

'Every mother wants the best. I wanted something different for you from what I had. I didn't want you making my mistakes.'

'You're dishonest.'

'Everyone is sometimes. We get on okay, you and I. We had some happy times.'

'I don't know you.'

"Course you do. I'm not any different. Don't be a what-ser-name . . . a prude. Suppose we might as well go to bed.'

The dog went on barking. Violet couldn't sleep. She lay thinking about what Eric had said about Spain. The Spanish were different about animals, they ignored them or made use of them, especially cats and dogs. No one felt sorry for them or bothered to like them. Even birds were kept for a purpose, in cages to bring good luck. The dogs sounded loudest just before daylight. They had six more days to go.

Ivy was up when she woke. Her bedspread was smooth, her nightdress out of sight. In the bathroom the towels were folded, the shower curtains pulled. On the rim of the bidet was her folded flannel under a piece of pink soap. Her washed tights hung over the bathtub, the new beaded dress was hung up. More scattered beads were piled in the soap dish. Ivy might be a cheat, faithless, a liar. She kept things in their right place.

Out on the veranda the cushions were tidied, the bottle and glasses were gone. Ivy's knitting was on the table, a half-knitted blue baby jacket. The leaves were still crushed where she'd leaned on them. Had she dreamed or imagined that hand? The morning was pale streaked, lovely, she'd always liked watching the sky. Low tide was a lonely time with the beach so bare. She'd never learned to swim, nor had Ivy, they didn't enjoy the splashing, shouting and wet. They liked the seaside for the gift shops, the ice cream kiosks and crowds. She looked across the bay for Ivy, perhaps she'd gone out for some tea. They'd forgotten to pack tea-bags.

Below the veranda, in the street, vans were delivering food. The kitchen staff were shouting. Men carried wooden trays of bread rolls and coarse sacks of green peppers. A garlic root rolled in the gutter. Green grapes in soft paper were lifted from basket skips. A boy hurled a hard pear at a driver. He lit a cigarette. From the Germans' room next door came coughing sounds. How much had they heard last night? And where was Ivy? The shore was empty but for the seaweed like pencil scribbles over the sand. A swimmer's head was bobbing near the red buoy far out to sea. She strained her eyes till they ached.

At the far side of the bay was the pedal boat man's hut. He rented out sun beds too, with mattresses and sun shades bleached pale in the salty glare. He came out of his hut, he had someone with him. Violet blinked and narrowed her lids. It was Ivy. Could it be Ivy? Up to her tricks again? Ivy disliked sunbathing, getting her skin burned from lying unclothed in the heat. It was Ivy with the pedal boat man with her arm around his neck. Had Spain sent Ivy mad?

'Ivee . . . Iv-eeee.'

She was too far away to hear. She could see the two of them talking, faces touching, she could see Ivy fondle his hair. He went into his hut again. Ivy walked towards the hotel.

The swimmer near the buoy was coming in, walking towards the sand. His thighs dripped, he shook himself, wiped the wet from his hairy chest. That shiny head, she knew it, he was the wine waiter, Jose.

Ivy saw him, she ran to him, she called to him. A dog behind her barked. The sun was so bright Violet's eyes watered, it was all unreal, a dream. Ivy had her arms round the wine waiter who'd come dripping in from the sea. The dog was barking round them, darting at Ivy's heels. Ivy was betraying Chester again with a wine waiter with hair shined like shoes. She was turning her back on marriage, on everything she upheld. She clung on to Jose while the dog barked and scuffled. Ivy was faithless, a toe-rag, she only loved herself.

She went into the bathroom. She longed to talk to someone, she felt lonely. Ches wasn't her Dad any more. She ran the bath taps and shower faucet. Which was real, the Ivy in Shadwell or the one in Spain? She'd heard that the sun here brought out weakness, in August the heat made you crazed. Ivy wasn't used to such excitement, she was used to their caravan. She wasn't used to being without Dad or hotel meals with champagne. She must protect Ivy, look after her, bring her safely back to Dad. She'd try not to criticize her again, they would enjoy themselves according to the original plan. Ivy needed a break as well as she did. She washed herself with pink soap.

'Hi, Vee. You missed a lovely walk. I been all round the front. The gardens are lovely.'

Violet wrapped towels round her. She stared at Ivy. Her eyes were bright, she looked excited, almost pretty with a smile like a girl. Her hair wasn't so curly, hanging loose round her face. She said Spain in the morning was beautiful, they'd have a happy day.

'Are you wet, Ivy? You been paddling? I saw you on the beach.'

'Not me. Just the gardens. It's lonely out on your own.'

'I saw you. I'm sure I did. With someone.'

'You were seeing things. I was in the garden in front. Look, here's a flower like a violet, a sort of Spanish one.'

Perhaps she'd been dreaming or imagining, like when she saw the hand. This plain pale Ivy couldn't be lying. She needed her even if she was. She supposed Ivy still needed her.

There was no sign of Jose at breakfast. You collected your own food from buffet tables in the dining-room. Hot rolls, coffee, fruit. There were smoked meats and cheeses if you were very hungry. She and Ivy thought alike about cheeses, especially Spanish ones, you didn't know from what animal's milk it came. Those smoked pink slices laid on plates might well be yesterday's bull, knifed to death in the sand. They drank their coffee at their same window table, spreading thick fruit conserve on the rolls.

'We'll buy tea-bags presently, won't we, Vee? And some condensed milk for our fridge. Coffee is nice, smells lovely. But give me a tea first thing.'

The German couple were enjoying cheese slices laid on pieces of tender pink meat. They dipped crusty bits of roll into their coffee and smiled. She was wearing a blouse with a bow on it. With camera and suntan oil, feeling rested and refreshed, they were ready for a day on the beach.

'We're off to the market ourselves now, the other end of the town. D'you fancy coming along with us? Just the four of us? Do.'

They refused Ivy's offer. No thank you. They wanted to rest in the sun. They had come here for sand and sea air, to get away from city crowds. Ivy said okay, suit theirselves, she and Vee liked a throng.

Now that Violet was going buying with Ivy their holiday was starting. She'd forget about last night and early morning. What Ivy did alone was her business, she'd never stop being her friend. They'd always loved shopping sprees, 'specially markets, where Dad used to pitch his stall. Ivy used to collect boxes and purses. They loved animal ornaments too, and joke toys. She'd had a clay cottage, you put a lit cigarette in it to make smoke out of the chimney. She'd had a rubber bun, real looking, with sugar and plastic peel. When you wound it up it became airborne, flying round the room on pretty transparent wings. She'd played with it till it broke. She'd never owned a doll or any kind of pet. She'd not had a close friend at school, that's why Dick had meant so much.

'Oh hurry, Vee, do. I'm dying to see what it's like.'

You could hear the market before you saw it. Shouting, whistling, dogs. More exciting than a London market, the people looked so foreign as well as the stuff they sold, and it smelled foreign. The local people did their shopping early, provisions for the day. The stalls were lined along two sides of the square, from each one came a different smell. The fish stalls were together in a corner, whitebait and strange glittering eels. There were baskets of live crabs and lobsters, as well as shark and squid.

'Look, birds, Vee. In those cages. Isn't that cruel.'

Ivy had the same look in her eyes as when she'd seen the bulls. How could people do that? Birds of all sizes were in cages too small for them stacked under a canvas awning. The pigeons, canaries and finches sat flat-eyed, dull and still. The cocks and hens couldn't turn if they wanted or even stretch their necks. The slatted wood cages had no feeding pots. Ivy and Violet looked away. Birds suffering from thirst, starving dogs, dying bulls were a part of the life here they must ignore. People in hot climates were different. Life was hard, work was scarce, it showed in their eyes. They didn't smile a lot, even the children looked grave, running the streets in dark overalls on their way to the nuns at school. Tourism was their livelihood, Spain was lovely, you ignored what you didn't like.

'Look at the leather. Spanish leather, handsewn. Cheap.'

'The purple bag is nice, Vee. Shaped into a cat.'

'I don't think it's leather. It's plastic. You have it, Ivy, I'll buy it for you.'

They turned over the sandals, smelling strongly in the sun. They looked at outsized rosaries with plastic crosses and Christs. Ivy wanted one for her bedroom and a leather bow for her hair. They forgot everything but the pleasure of buying, they'd spend their pesetas here.

Ivy bought a shaver for Chester that played tunes when you plugged it in. One stall had a lot of joke toys, that played or lit up when you pressed. There were umbrellas that banged like pop guns, there were yoyos and barking cigars. Violet bought a leather lampshade embroidered with curious beads.

'Look, Vee. Shoes with flowers on them. Just the thing for a holiday.'

Should they choose roses, violets or daisies? All English flowers but Violet, on looking closer, said the shoes were made in Wolverhampton, they weren't Spanish at all. Made of rubber, they were beach shoes, they would wear them after their baths. Violet bought white ones and Ivy some pale mauve; they got caps to match with rubber flowers over the ears. They found a stall that sold tea-bags. Another sold Spanish buns. They bought slabs of nougat, dotted with cherries and nuts. Not knowing Spanish didn't matter, they pushed, they pointed, they smiled. They kept catching each other's eye.

'Over there, oh my lor', Vee, I'd like to buy Ches one of those.'

'Those are lovely, Ivy. Charmian might like them.'

They avoided the bird stall on the way back again, they walked along the shore wearing their beach shoes, their other shoes dangling over their wrists by the heel straps. The sand was hot now, the sun beds were filling up. Brown bodies of the tourists lay quietly, limbs shining with oils and creams. Like breadloaves, Ivy said, only greasier. The pedal boat man clinked his bag. Had Violet imagined him earlier? Was it a trick of the light? Watching down from their balcony was much better than walking here.

'Look Vee, the Germans. Over there.'

Side by side, sun beds touching, the couple looked like one shape. Pressed like dough, lips seeking, the woman wriggled her toes. The man's trunks wouldn't pull up, his paunch pushed the waistband down. Her bikini had caught in the fold of her buttock. The oil they had rubbed over their bodies had smeared across the beds. Ivy said such weight was dangerous and that kissing in this heat gave you germs. Sand and seaweed bred infection, anyone knew that. This sun was enough to give you nightmares, they'd be okay in their room.

'Happy there, dears, are you? We been to the market ourselves.'

The Germans didn't answer, they were too busy with love in the sun.

Their room was a cool welcome, the air conditioner hummed. The chamber maids had left fresh linen, their beds were glassy smooth. First they rinsed their toes under the shower before putting the shoes on again. They washed with fresh pieces of pink soap, marbled with glycerine. They drew the curtains to seal out the heat before they settled to look at their things. There was more of the soap for Charmian, and fine handkerchiefs edged with lace. Charmian had behaved worse than a shoplifter but she was decent underneath. Ivy liked her. She'd bought a pretty fan for her with bulls on it, for Eric she chose two leather ties. They admired the huge rosary, Ivy hung it over a chair. They tried on their new dark glasses as well as the bathing caps. They ate some crisps. Ivy said timidly that she was getting the hang of Spain now, she was beginning to unwind. Was there anything Vee would like rinsed through, not to hang on the veranda but over the bathroom rail?

'I can do that, Ivy. Or the chambermaid. You mustn't wait on me here.'

'I'm your mother, I want things to be right with us. Like it was before.'

'You can't just wish away last night, Ivy. What you told me isn't a small thing.'

'I know. I wish I hadn't now.'

'You seeing Joe tonight?'

'Oh not again. He's not working today anyway. I got a bit carried away yesterday. I'm too old for that sort of thing.'

No more was said about Joe or the pedal boat man. It had all been muddled and sad. They would rest now until lunchtime. Ivy's ankle hurt. She'd tripped and bruised it early this morning.

CHAPTER FIFTEEN

Chester

'I can't hear you, Vi'let. It's a bad line. Vi'let?'

'Dad . . . Dad, it's about Ivy.'

'Eh? What's that? Speak up. Let me talk to Ivy.'

'She . . . she's . . .'

'Speak louder, Vi'let. I'm missing you both a lot. It seems ages . . .'

'Dad . . . Ivy . . . a dog bit her . . .'

'What's that?'

'She was bitten . . . she . . .'

'What dog, Vi'let? Don't fool around. Hello?' He shook the receiver, he banged the instrument. Dead as a corpse. 'Hello?'

He must get hold of Ivy. Trust those Spanish phones. 'Dog bite'? What did she mean? 'Course they did have those wild dogs in Spain, running about on the stray. Vi'let's voice sounded funny. He should never have let them go. Ivy would have it, and what Ivy wanted she got. All because of Vi'let, naturally. No peace since she got back. That cat was out of the way at any rate. But he still felt low in himself. It was so quiet without Ivy. Later in the year he'd take her to a caravan, after he'd recovered from Spain. The holiday for the two had cleaned him out. He and Ivy liked a simple holiday, but she must have her Spain with her Vee. He'd been afraid Vi'let's marriage wouldn't work out. Like getting silk from a pig's ear. Impossible. Eric was born to the purple, Vi'let was a Shadwell girl. If Vi'let had stayed single she and Ivy would be safe at

131

home now. She wouldn't be ringing from the other side of nowhere with some story about a dog. Ivy would know what to do all right, but he ought to be there too. He and Ivy were like one person, he clung and she clung back. A call from the continong was quite an event all the same; she'd get through again when she could. He'd keep busy while he waited.

He fetched a broom from the broom cupboard. Everything was spotless, Ivy's floors always were. He wasn't used to indoor sweeping, only dealing with the market pitch at the end of the day. Linoleum felt different. He'd get a cloth out after, give the whole place a bit of a lick. That call shouldn't be long coming through now. 'Course a dog bite could be a painful thing . . . This polish smelled nice and fresh. He'd rub over the bathroom too, nothing like elbow grease. You could reach right underneath these zinc baths behind their claw feet. Only yesterday Ivy had been sitting in it, singing and rubbing her back. He could smell her highlight shampoo still. She'd been like a kid, with her new clothes for the trip, getting her roots touched up, buying light luggage for the plane. Vi'let had been the quiet one, though the whole thing was her idea. Vi'let had changed since she got back here, though just as lazy and rude. Gone quiet now, spending too much time in bed. She'd let her looks go, though her hair was a lot better without that coloured stuff. Just because she was expecting didn't mean she shouldn't care. Expectancy wasn't a disease. She'd been high-handed with Charmian, landing her with that cat. He didn't complain, he couldn't be doing with Dick. He'd footed the Spanish bill, it had left him stony, though.

He finished off the bathroom, he'd scoured the sink and taps. He'd check their cooker next because Ivy had trouble with that. She had a spray-cleaner for where she couldn't reach. She had nice hands, Ivy had, small ones. Granted their oven was old, cast iron was made to last. He needed her. He sprayed into the corners, where her fingers couldn't curve. He shivered . . . You'd think after all that energy he'd feel warmer. His arms ached now, not from the work but from needing Ivy. She was out of his reach for a week, it was natural to feel cold. The bed was so cold alone, he'd not been able to sleep. He liked dropping off feeling her feet on his, liked feeling her bleachy hair. Her bottom was lovely to cuddle and nothing he did was wrong. If you loved and knew each other there was no end to ways of love. His only secret was that he'd never given her a child. He couldn't, due to mumps as a teenager. Violet wasn't his, he'd let Ivy believe he thought so. Nothing Ivy did was wrong; their kind of love stood any test.

He'd keep the flat shining till she got back. There'd be some straight talking to do. Eric wasn't facing up to his duties, not as a man or a husband. Someone would need to take charge. Where was Vi'let to live? With who and when would she go . . .? What had she meant, 'dog bite'? Pets were a nuisance from beginning to end. They bit, they smelled, they messed, they caused allergies to humans. He'd have thought the bites Ivy most risked were the ones he gave her himself, on her tit-ends or on her back-side, where she hoped Vi'let wouldn't see. She worried about Vi'let overhearing them, always the same from when she was a kid . . . Vi'let should ask the courier to help them, they were paid for it, practical and medical aid. There were injections for bites. He'd try and put a call through from this end, via the continental exchange. He'd never done that before. A snooty voice told him there was a three-hour delay.

'Please put me through now. I must talk to my wife. She's been taken queer.'

'I'm sorry, caller, there is a three-hour delay. Do you wish me to book the call?'

'Put me through, please. I must talk.'

Flaming 'eck, didn't she understand English? Now, not in three hours' time. That class of person fancied they ruled the earth. He ought to report her, he was too upset just now. She sounded worse than Lady How-Now Charmian. Of course, *she* would help him. Another person's posh accent wouldn't trouble Charmian, she'd tell that operator where she belonged. Look up the C. Caive-Propp number.

'Mr Stubbs, Chester? How delightful to hear your voice. I've been meaning to contact you, to ask after your absent ones.'

'Eh? What's that?'

'The Spanish holiday-makers. I was wondering if you'd care to take supper here, one evening after your work?'

'It's about my Ivy, see.'

'Dear person, we became acquainted before she left. She's a remarkable woman, I look forward to her return.'

'Our Vi'let has rung up from Spain. She's . . . there's been a bit of bother, see, and Ivy's been taken queer.'

'What is it? Too much sun, Chester?'

'Something about . . . Vi'let didn't actually say, we got cut off, see. I don't know what . . .'

He knew she'd offer to help, her class had the know-how. She wouldn't let herself be cut off. 'Course he blamed Vi'let for a lot of it, she showed no more sense than a cat.

He went into the front room, he'd wait there till Charmian called back. Funny how dead it smelled in there. It wasn't used, that was why. Last time he'd been in there was Christmas, with the tree and holly and cards. Just the two of them, except for Boxing Day when Vi'let came, as happy as kids on their own.

He looked out at the darkness, the sky was black as smoke. They got a lot of smoke or fog round Shadwell, being low-lying at the mouth of the Thames. Spring was slow coming this year, he was lucky, snow didn't bother him. It bothered Ivy and Vi'let. He liked to think of them sunning themselves while he kept the place ready for them here. Once Dick was off the premises his sneezing and scratching had stopped. Lady Charmian was welcome to him.

He put a duster over the oil stove that was hardly ever used.

All that heat in the house on the green hadn't improved Vi'let's nature, she still had a vile mouth. She never got that from him or Ivy, he didn't like women to swear. He dusted the sill and window ledges. He looked at the tree by the lighted bus stop, with the rubbish at its roots. There were bus tickets, crisp bags, dogs' mess, but not flowers like Ivy saw. She must have bad sight else how did she see snowdrops? Perhaps she saw what she wanted to see. She liked looking up at the heavens, they were both optimists in their way. They were alike in so many things, that's why he was worried sick now. Not knowing was worse than knowing. Knowing what? He still felt cold. When he got the carpet sweeper it spat out a trail of dust. Then the door bell rang.

'Chester? May I come in? I came here as soon as I could. I thought I would come in person instead of telephoning.'

'What? Eh?'

'Thank you, my dear. What a cosy little home you have. We got through on the exchange, got a connection. I . . . we . . . spoke to Violet.'

'Ivy? Did you speak to her?'

'I'm afraid that was not possible. You see, my dear, it is bad news.'

'I know.'

He'd known all the time, he'd known inside, when Vi'let rang. Pain felt worse when you knew there was no escape from it, when you had to accept the truth. No more waiting, not knowing, not letting yourself believe. He'd guessed when Vi'let first rang and spoke to him. He'd known for certain when he'd looked at the tree. Bus tickets, and mess, not snowdrops. Smoke and fog, not the stars. Charmian was standing in his passage telling him what he'd known. The pain inside him was real now, in his chest, in his throat, in his eyes. He couldn't accept it from Vi'let, he'd guessed what she tried to tell. He couldn't see Ivy no more now, not alive, not again. He was alive, Ivy wasn't.

He stared into Charmian's eyes. What was she talking about now? She could leave now, go away, she'd said what she'd come to say, no point in her standing about. What soft hair she had, like white silk.

'Beg pardon, what did you say?'

'Eric, my son, is back in England. I have been expecting him. I didn't have a chance to tell you earlier.'

'Eh?'

'Eric helped me to ascertain the situation in Spain. And my dear . . . it's bad.'

'I know.'

'Ivy was bitten. She died. Eric is leaving immediately, flying from Gatwick. He'll arrange the . . . formalities. Afterwards he'll bring Violet home. It's all a great shock, I do extend my sympathy.'

'What's Eric got to do with it? It's my wife, Ivy is mine.'

'The . . . formalities. Please, Chester, Eric knows best.'

'It's my daughter and my wife you're talking about. Take your nose out of it. It's our business, it isn't yours.'

'Please, Chester, please.'

'If it hadn't been for your Eric none of this would have been.'

'Don't torture yourself. Here, Chester, come and sit down.'

'I'll do as I please. I'll stand.'

'I am a part of this tragedy, part of the family. I was beginning to like Ivy, I was taking to her.'

'Not Ivy. Not my Ivy.'

'My dear.'

'Why? Why? Why her?'

'Death is no respecter of persons. I know. I have known it too.'

'How could you understand it? You're different. You're out of another world.'

'Pain makes little distinction. We all feel pain, we all react.'

She had the answer, the knowledge, the way of putting it. He couldn't go to Spain at once anyway, he'd no passport and not much cash. She didn't know what real living was but she knew about death. She was superior, clickey, posh. He needed her.

She spoke quietly to him. She told him that Ivy had picked up an infection called tetanus. He'd heard of that. If not treated immediately it could be fatal. They had inoculated Ivy with serum, they hadn't been quick enough. The bacillus, found in soil usually, entered abrasions or cuts. In Ivy's case it was a small scratch, from a dog probably. Contamination in hot countries was rife. They would hear more when Eric arrived there.

'You mean a post mortem. I won't have it. I'm not having Ivy cut.'

'We must just be patient at this point, Chester.'

He nodded. He saw the wisdom. You had to obey the law. Charmian was trying to be helpful, she'd known loss too in her way. But nobody could feel this amount of pain and go on living. Help me, Ivy, I can't manage alone. There's no life here without you, no point to it.

He was being rude to Charmian. Ivy hated rudeness. If she were here she'd be making Charm welcome, she always treated guests well. She was an East-ender, whatever you had you shared.

'You turned out very late to come here, Charmian. I'm sorry I was a bit rude. I'd run you home in my van only it's in being serviced. It's foggy to be out alone.'

He turned the oven flame to high. Ivy would offer tea and sandwiches, or send out for some beer. Charmian most likely didn't bother watching the telly, he'd offer her wine if he could.

'You could stop the night here if you've a mind to. In Vi'let's room.' He explained about the bathroom being near her, she was very welcome to stay. Being an early riser he used the kitchen sink himself.

There wasn't a lot more to say then. She was right, they

137

must be patient and wait. He tried to tell her he was grateful. She put out her soft little hand. Don't mention it, a pleasure, as good as the queen she was, a queen without her gloves. She wasn't a lot more comfort than the queen, but she meant well, she had a heart.

He was glad of somebody in the other room, better than being quite alone. He had all his life for aloneness. He lay in their big bed. Not 'their' room now, or 'their' bed. He'd have to learn to say 'his'.

'Ivy? Darl?'

He took her pillow and hugged it, wiping his face on it, smelling her 'Woodland Whisper', saying her name again.

'Darl.'

CHAPTER SIXTEEN

Eric and Violet

'I think it went well, Violet. What did you think?'

Violet said that she worried most about Chester. He'd looked so sad and old, trying to follow the mass for his dead wife. What had grieved him most was the penny-pinching and economy. He felt the shame of Ivy being buried in Spain and not in Shadwell because of the cost of embalming, the cost of air freight. They weren't even insured.

Eric had done the best he could. After America he was short of money himself. The Spanish authorities had insisted on speed. Because of the heat, he supposed. He had telephoned Chester asking for money urgently. Chester had choked with grief into the receiver. Ivy's Spanish trip had cleaned him out. There had been no alternative. Ivy was buried in a small graveyard outside the town on the side of a barren brown hill. The rigidity of the Spanish bureaucracy surprised him. To them a death was failed tourism, no one welcomed it, it made a mark on the wrong side of their business. A dead Catholic was marginally more welcome than a dead non-Catholic. There was no precedent for any rite other than Catholic rites. She had had a Catholic interment conducted with cavalier speed. It was fortunate that Chester hadn't been present, he'd been spared the shame of the grave on the bare hillside with none of the flowers she had loved except for Violet's posy. The requiem mass back in London was a gesture of atonement. They had honoured her soul today. Though but a half-hearted believer she would have approved. Yes, the mass had gone quite well.

During the service his thoughts kept returning to Spain. When he'd arrived at the Excelsior Violet had been packing Ivy's things. She had been holding a horrific purple garment with a broken beaded fringe. Ivy had been wearing it when the ambulance took her, when her bitten ankle swelled. She'd run a high fever before the final spasm, when her throat and jawbone froze. Dead two hours later. Diamond, the courier, had gone with Violet to the hospital, though her professional cheer had dimmed. No allowance was made for death on a package tour, it lowered the tone of the trip. Clients reacted adversely, their search for the sun was dulled. Diamond had asked Violet not to talk of it, it might bring the tour more bad luck.

Violet had been quite admirable, quietly packing those clothes that still smelled of that woodland scent Ivy favoured. For the first time since he'd known Violet she wasn't wearing scent. She looked different, her face was washy pale, her hair dark and straight, no jewellery, just her wedding ring. Her beautiful rinsed blue eyes hadn't changed though and they were in Spain again. The dress that she was folding had stains under the arms, the bead braiding was hanging loose. She was so beautiful. Had she got knickers on? She'd touched him and he couldn't help himself, didn't consider if the time was suitable, he'd pulled down her dark dress and kissed her. Her moist mouth, her neck and warm hair. Her kisses smelled of garlic and toothpaste, her jutting eye tooth pressed his lip. Her eyes were wet, with wet lashes. He had kissed them and tasted the salt. The same bedroom, the same bathroom and veranda. There were rosary beads on the floor. He had her back on to the same pillows. Later again on the veranda, with cushions on the same tiles. 'Hush, darling, we'll be overheard.' Afterwards they lay talking. She told him everything that had happened while he wrote on the skin of her back. She told him about the German couple, the friends that Ivy hoped to make. When he asked her if she could forgive him she'd told him not to be daft.

They had gone together to the various officials to sign forms and documents produced by cold-eyed upholders of the law. They were together again after loving in their rooms in the Excelsior. After it was all over they could go back there again.

So they had returned to Chester and Charmian.

At the requiem mass this morning they had sat in a quiet row, trying to pray prayers that they neither knew nor understood that would comfort Ivy's soul. Chester, in his brown pinstripe suit, broke down again, weeping in his large-knuckled hands. Charmian put a small handkerchief to her eyes mourning her newly-made friend who had bought her a fan patterned with bulls and had knitted cleverly for the coming child. She would miss her. Eric grieved for his unusual mother-in-law who had bought him two leather ties and left Violet to his care. Violet had done her crying in Spain. She stared at the priest, the same man who had married them, with large clear brilliant eyes. The four of them had stood up and sat down appropriately, crossing themselves with unsure hands. They had wondered about bowing the knee on leaving and entering the pew and what to do about the holy water. Yes, the service had gone well.

Back at the 'Purple Rest' kitchen they'd grown closer over the simple meal that Eric and Violet had prepared earlier. Cold salmon which Charmian enjoyed, a green salad with avocados, followed by apple pie and cream. Chester ate the apple pie heartily, the icing sugar had flecked his tie. Coffee from the percolator was served in purple mugs. There was no mention of the dining-room or the missing furniture. There was plenty of time for change. He and Violet were together again. Taste was arbitrary. It changed with changing times.

'Yes, it did go well.'

'More sherry?'

'No ta. I never liked it, 'specially being pregnant now. Nice of Charm to get those new decanters.'

'She shouldn't have acted as she did in this house. I really had no idea, Violet.'

'I shouldn't have gone to Spain. Ivy would be alive . . . if . . . I wish I'd never gone.'

'I felt abominable, not bringing back her body, because of going to the States.'

'It was up to Chester too. Poor Chester, it's worst for him.'

'He enjoyed the service, I think. And the lunch. Here, we can save these pears.'

She covered the dish with plastic, made space in the salad tray. The fridge was neat and well stocked now. She said that Chester had told her that she should make 'Purple Rest' into a home. Until now it was just a house. Did Eric understand?

'I think I do. We'll try, shall we?'

'I've been pretty rotten. Pretty much of a toe-rag.'

'Don't say that. Are you adjusting now?'

'Adjusting? What do you mean? Talk English, can't you?'

'I mean the child. Your baby, and mine too.'

'I didn't want it. I hate kids. If it's there then it's there, I suppose.'

He said that they'd both feel differently when they had it.

'Yeah. Suppose you're right. Eric, what about that play you were doing? In America. I forgot to ask.'

He explained then in a quiet voice that the play didn't exist. He had come back without even the outline. It was too late now to enter the competition, he'd never get it done. His plan was a dream, his journey a mistake.

'You'll have to go on being a teach then, won't you? If I'm having this baby you will. Shame really . . . Still . . .'

'There may be other chances. I've not given up all hope.'

'Till we have built Jerusalem, in England's green and pleasant land.' Yes, there was hope.

'We know each other a bit better, after this lot, anyway. Perhaps the four of us could go away somewhere, not Spain I mean, for a break?'

'We could. Shall we?'

'I read somewhere about a TV documentary called "The Secrets of Family Love". It's different episodes and sections. Like marriage, bereavement, birth. Families are invited to appear, to take part in it. D'you fancy it, Eric? We could write in, find out more.'

'We could. We might. Shall we?'